ANGELIC KREATIONS
Poetry Between Sisters

Karen Yelverton

ANGELIC POETRY
Poetry Between Sisters

HOV Publishing a division of HOV, LLC.
www.hopeofvisionpublishing.com
hopeofvision@gmail.com

Cover Design: Marrio Marshall
Front Cover Photography Credit: Thomas Brice
Back Cover and Inside Group Photo Credit: Theron Tee-Smith
Editor/Proofreader: Bettye Walker

Write the Author Karen Yelverton at:
Email: kyelve18@gmail.com

For more information about special discounts for bulk purchases, please contact kyelve18@gmail.com or hopeofvision@gmail.com

ISBN: 978-1-942871-22-4
Library of Congress Control Number: 2017932345

10 9 8 7 6 5 4 3 2 1

Printed in the United States of America

DEDICATION

It's an honor and privilege to dedicate this book to three people who have had a tremendous influence in my life my mother: *Betty Yelverton Quashie* who gave her all to ensure I was able to set forth to attain my visions, dreams and goals; mommy you are the anchor of my soul.

My sister *Adrianne Renee Tart* who has always been truthful, uplifting with unconditional love and never judged me. Thank you for your loyalty it's astonishing.

My "CHAMP" uncle *Aaron Yelverton* for setting me back on the right path, reinforcing my love and compassion for life, and the necessity to help others.

ACKNOWLEDGEMENTS

I have been blessed with a phenomenal support team who understands my vision and willingly joined me on this Amazing journey. I am grateful to my brother Thomas Brice; East New York to ATL, told you your work would be seen and admired worldwide. My graphic artist Marrio Marshall; over eighteen years of friendship, working together bringing the best out of my work every time. Theron Tee-Smith thanks for sharing your talent, time and expertise. The sisters and I are ready, willing and able for the next journey.

Special Thanks to Lenny Luv, the sisters and brothers at Man Up Inc., my LEO friend Rhonda Brown Moore who led the path to HOV Publishing, LLC. "you are an amazing resource", along with Mykala and HOV publish. I am looking forward to more great life changing ventures. To all my life coaches, mentors along with those I have coached and mentored…you all have blessed me with life changing lessons and I truly thank you.

For the lives lost in this book I stay strong and write for you. For the lives still breathing in fresh air, I dare you to soar higher each day. Thanks to my incredible Angelic Poets and Artists…I could not do what I do without you. Together we are changing lives and making a positive impact in the world. "I heart you".

Karen "KK" Yelverton

TABLE OF CONTENTS

FOREWORD

Not only is it a pleasure, it is an honor to have been given the opportunity to write the Foreword for *Angelic Kreations: Poetry Between Sisters*. I was a bit confused about where to begin since I am a brother and not a sister. Then it suddenly dawned on me as I reflected on the images Karen has illuminated in this inaugural collection: As a man in millennial America poised to make a difference, it is paramount that I listen to the voices of my Sisters.

Since birth, my life has been molded and shaped by Sisterhood. My mother was the first Sister I encountered. She showed me love and taught me discipline. Karen displays her love and discipline, not only in the form of the unleashed wisdom of her ancestors but also by introducing us to the state of mind of our newest generation, through the writings of the students that have contributed to *Angelic Kreations*.

Angelic Kreations energized me to "study" that which I did not know and to "act" upon that which I do know. Karen's boldness on paper and in the flesh is infectious and empowering making this a must read for all sexes and races. Karen Yelverton's form of "edutainment," as represented on the pages of this current manifesto, serves as a flashlight to guide us through the tunnel of knowns and unknowns. The human race depends on it.

I love the title of this work because it is so reflective of the author. Karen is truly an angel without wings, who daily promotes the well being of the Family and Sisterhood. As an educator, she has the daily opportunity to speak directly to our next generation and offer them hope and instruction for the future. She herself is transformed daily into a student, learning from those she has been assigned to teach.

As a poet, Karen speaks boldly and unapologetically about issues that affect our world as a whole. Her noble, regal presence is an example and beacon for all mankind and more specifically, WOMANKIND.

I hope *Angelic Kreations: Poetry Between Sisters* starts the first day of the rest of your life with hope. It definitely did for me and I will never be the same.

Shamello Durant
Music Producer
Producers Coalition of America

INTRODUCTION

As fresh water meanders its way along a stream so is the breath of fresh air that exudes in this book of poetry.

The poets, who are mostly young women have experienced and still are experiencing some form of struggle. This is their way of speaking from their hearts and giving meaning to their dreams and triumphs.

As the principal poet, I have overcome obstacles that have resulted in life changing perspectives. The thoughts in my poems are my way of addressing these issues, while at the same time teaching and encouraging women of all ages to pen their thoughts and let their wisdom be glistening stars.

The poets' efforts are greatly applauded. This is only the beginning of greater works to come. As you read, reflect and experience true life, it is the dawn of a new day for all involved including you, the reader!

VISIONS, DREAMS AND GOALS

Vision, Dream and Goals
You are in Control and it's time to manifest
Your "Visions Dreams and Goals"
For the Father up above has given our Kings the tools
Allowing Queens like you
To carry a child in your womb

Giving birth to this new generation
That has been sanctioned to forget
their "Visions Dreams and Goals"

So it's left up to us to entrust
In each other and every Sister and Brother to your left and right
In spite of the differences we may face
It's time to uplift putting forth our best efforts to fight
Stopping Racism and White Supremacy
Not with HATE Education, self-preservation
Stop and think for one second
What are your Visions, Dreams and Goals?
The one thing we have in common
Are our Visions, Dreams and Goals and
The need to plant a seed, watch it grow and succeed

Against all odds it's not hard
If we all work together
Becoming masters at weathering storms
Queens like us can and will keep things calm
We hold the victory it's in our history
Sometimes hidden deep down in our souls,

But your goals meet your visions in your dreams
And although we may see and experience negativity
It's the passion for your goals
That allows your visions to dream

Aiming higher to inspire
And educate an entire planet
The Here the Now and the Afterlife
Let's just not get together but love one another
Working together

Time to refine and refrain
From crabs in a bucket that can cut like a knife
We are the first creators it's true
It's time to fight
With Love, Education, Research, Reading, Patience,
Self-Reflection and Self- Preservation

It starts with self
Always remember
they are Your "Visions, Dreams & Goals"
And no one else

So take them and cherish them daily
Watching them Manifest and Grow
Because like SANDRA BLAND
Only you will truly know!!
If you've given your very BEST!!

EMPOWERMENT

Empowerment
Your Improvement
Your Movement
To open up your minds
Stand Strong
Stand Tall

Ladies, Queens and Goddesses it's time
To shape your future
Attain to obtain your goals
Only you can stop yourself

Let your vision shine
Shine brighter than the brightest diamond or ruby
It's your inner beauty
Only you can stop yourself

Allowing a person, place or process
To distract you from life's pleasures
While haters measure
How and why
We do what we do

Never will they be able to walk a mile in our shoes
Jazzeppi's, Red Bottoms, Jeffrey Campbell's and Yeezy's
It's an everyday struggle
How we maintain our hustle

We go so hard
Holding down the universe
Giving praises daily
Thanks be to God

We smile knowing we will never
Receive or get our just due accolades
But we keep moving forward
Knowing our blessings are to come

From the youth that speak the truth
Watch their lights shine
Shine Brighter than a diamond
On the hand of a woman
Who used to be banned from doing just about whatever
But we stand tall
Defeating all the odds together

As a group we can empower communities
With common unity
Empowerment can be taken to another level
Involving, evolving and building trust
In cooperation and positive communication
Between one another
There is a prerequisite for this

Structure, protocols, procedures in place
Sanctioned against those who abuse
Or choose to loose
Between you, and me
We are responsible for creating opportunities
For sisters to meet and greet
Share opinions and views
Having fun celebrating life with one another

I wasn't put on this earth to only work and pay
bills My ancestry runs too deep
I have miraculous healing power tools
So don't be fooled
With the words I spit
It's time to empower
'Cause we were destined to be here without fear

Lil Moe, Tashera Simmons, Karmen,
Sharonda, Gail and Kindra Ladies,
let's toast and say cheers!

HELLO FEBRUARY

So much history hidden
Must be revealed since your existence
Carter G. Woodson
Must pay homage with a moment in silence
Sir Hotep, I am honored

Let's start by understanding there was a plan
For February in celebration of the Black man
President Abraham Lincoln's born day
Along with Frederick Douglass
Played a role in why February was chosen

Formally known as the **"Negro History Week"**
To bring attention to his mission and help school systems
We have always been in demand
With a book and plan in hand
So please stop with the ignorant conversations
We have a lot of work to do around this nation

Distractions have you distracted
Unable to look beyond to see the factors
Deliberately poisoning water with celebrity bailouts
Ya'll worrying about men with hair pieces and Oscar statues
When you should be researching
Those not frequently on the news

Bernie Sanders unlabeled and unreported
Most extorted for their wisdom and knowledge
Like all the times they refused to label the KKK a terrorist mob

In existence since hate met evil
Millions hung while they stood in celebration
When the facts document who was the first creation

I'm tired of being patient
With these baby steps
While killing our babies across America
Satan showing no remorse or respect
So they tend to neglect
But instead on the negative they reflect
Created by those responsible for cutting the checks
To improve the conditions
So he thinks its best
To represent with his gun to get respect
But instead takes the wrong life
Now two families are left stressed

Trying to figure out and decide their next move
Should they stay or move out the
neighborhood To think this all took place
'Cause in class they couldn't prove
Who was the illest dude

On the block who stuck up kids like "Smooth"
But Smooth wanted no beef just went to school
To perform Desmond Tutu for Black history month
A humanitarian he admired and looked up to
Finding out later on they hit the wrong dude

One moment of silence: PAUSE
Enough Willie Lynch examples
Time over let's do what's right
So much to be proud of

So many unknown she-roes and heroes to explore
Sharing with our loved ones while we tour
This and every Black history moment in history

Turning off the negativity on social media
Radio and tell-a-lie vision
Reading, researching, enlightening and learning

Educating yourself or someone else
Armed ready mentally to take on the distractions
Not to self-destruct
While our ancestors have proven our strength
The baton has been passed on to us

Trust in yourself to make a difference
To many suffered, to many died
To many unknown graves
Not to attempt making a bigger and better difference
You will never know until you try

EARTH DAY CELEBRATION 2016

The year was '74
When the Spirits of GOD allowed me to
arrive On this very day - my earth day
My mother gave birth to a Matriarch
Granting me the vision to explore
Life, Love, Loyalty, Trust, Faithfulness

The need to help others
An important deed Planting Seeds
A quality I saw in Each of You
As I grew into a Queen and Matriarch
From Brooklyn

Never to be mistucken, excuse me, mistaken
For a Fake or Phony
Sometimes lonely
But a mother's wisdom and strength will always prevail

Life lessons told through their experiences, stories
Narratives and tales

Hazel, having you in my life during my early years
Set a strong Godly foundation big sis still till this day

Janet, I will always look up to you
Appreciating your guidance along the way

Venus, Stacey, Nikki you are a part of me
We never forgot what it took to get us here
From my heart to yours We All We Got
Uplifting supporting one another We Can Never Stop
The 857 family sister bond stands strong

Osie, Chance and L Brother, Father figure, Mentor all in one
Father, Nephew, Son
A package created especially for me look how far we have come

Cleavon, your friendship and caring heart
Keeps us bonded and will never tear us apart

Sonia, what can I say?
You were just meant to be a special part of our lives
A neighbor who became family
And someone who truly cares
Your willingness to always extend a helping hand
We appreciate you sooo much
I hope you understand the love is real
Just look at my best friend she'll be shedding a tear soon
Unless she laughs to shake it off and keeps still

Adriane Renee Tart, big part of my heart
Taught me at age five, how to share at Ernie's Pizzeria
They had the best pies
Beef patties, cold sodas and Italian ice "umm"

They showed us love there
Ok, so I get that she bribed me with food
Showing me the true meaning of sisterhood
With her by my side I always knew
I could fly and soar to the highest level
Of whatever I put my mind to
Hey my sis and I multi-talented
Just humbly speaking the truth

Dennis, my lil brother from 857
Grandma is smiling down on us with **Meka Luv**
And **Aunt Sallie** from heaven
Watching the family grow warms my heart
Love you to the moon and back my dear
Through good and bad near or far I'll be here

Mommy, are you happy to see everyone
This whole entire night is dedicated to you
Strongest bravest WOMAN walking this planet

Mommy, I love and truly adore you
Thanks for giving me a chance to breathe fresh air
Your only daughter,
I hope you are proud of the Woman I became
The woman you gave birth to and raised

A single mom who's superb
The Lord only knows where your strength comes from
I'm just blessed and thankful it's there
Never to be over looked or taken for granted
Camp Hurley's honor I swear.

HEY BEAUTIFUL

Hey beautiful Black queen
Do you know your worth and what it means?
To wear the color of your skin
Melanin rich body, bust, legs and butt
Some with thin and thick lips

They want to fool you and play tricks
Make you think you're not truly the God
Blissfully balanced in brilliance and bravery
Stop believing we began and came from slavery

You mothered earth from the birth of its foundation
As God's gift and God's creation
You were chosen to carry and care for life
Nine months in the womb
Some premature being a little impatient
Filled with the task of beautifying the world
Growing inside of you
Demanding your time, love and patience
Caring and understanding
Women are blessed
With the blossoming bonus of birthing a human life
Ready to take flight
Being watched through a microscopic light

And I know it's hard at times for you to understand
Consistently under attack
Music, movies, entertainment
Political issues and views
Religion and education
We are negatively labeled with negative reviews
Making it difficult to choose

When they calling us worthless b*tches and ho's
It's not just all on you
To avoid repetition
Proactively listening,
You're told to be tough Suck it up
Because life gets rough blinding others from seeing
The beautiful queen in you

'Cause we have been following
"Ameri-kkkan.." beauty standards and qualifications
When their definition of beauty needs an explanation

I don't usually name names
But this is for the sake of our youth
Demanding to know the truth
Asking why the Kardashian's get so much attention
Along with Scarlett Johansson, Jessica Beil,
Jennifer Lawrence and Megan Fox
Named the 2015 standards of what's HOT

NOT when you have the likes of beautiful queens
Like Taraji P. Henson, Sista Souljah, Gabrielle Union,
Kee Kee Palmer, Erica Badu, Jill Scott, Janelle Monae,
Kerry Washington, Kelly Rolland, Tatyana Ali,
Queen Latifah, Halle Berry, Rhianna, Solange and "B"

Beauty comes in all shapes, colors and sizes
Trust me, if you close your eyes
Try and imagine a world without you
The beauty of your bold and bubbling self
Brightening this dark world with the presence of your
Smile, Your style, your swag, your laughter on display
Your Happiness makes them mad
Questioning how you do what you do
Accomplishing any and everything you put your mind to

I have met so many beautifully blessed, brilliantly blazing and beyond
breathtaking fabulous women of color. Let me name a few:
• Adrianne • Venus • Stacey • Meka Luv (how I miss you) • Onika
• Marisol • Angie • Lena Soul • Rhonda • Meda • O • Toya • Nadia
• Misha • Ray-Ray • Delta • Marjorie • Mama Marg • Danielle
• Angelic Poets • Sonia • Christina • Karen • Brandi • Sissy
• Sarita • Mama Lynn • Mia • Imani • Crys C. • Charlene
• Kee Kee • Keich • Hazel • Janet • Sharonda • Natalie
• Dr. Doris • Judy • Julia • Krystal • Shana • Misa • Sylvia • Kyasha
• Carmen • Sister's Group • Kanitra • Cleta • Mama Barnes
• Aunty Less • Natalie • Mesh • Gina • Mrs. Rhasool and (You)
• Ms. Chase • Jennifer • Kecia • Women of F.D.A • SAPIS Women
• Aunt Claudette • Cousin Coutney • Big Mama Tash
• and ULEA you are one of them too!

Beauty is a state of mind
What you see in the mirror is mirrored by what's in your mind
Be extraordinary better than expected
Go beyond fabulous
Because in my eyes,
Sisters
I see nothing but beauty!!

LADY BUG

To The Ancestors I Feel In My Spirit Daily

I saw a lady bug crawling on my wall today
I said, "Hey, lady bug!"
How did you get your claim to fame?
Who gave you your name?

With your dark red skin and your sexy blacks dots
Placed perfectly all in the right spots
Crawling and flying around like you do
It is the beauty in you
That makes others have no clue
Of how much we actually have in common.

But I have a question for you, Lady Bug
How do you withstand, in front or behind your man?
Are you treated unfairly because of your dark red skin
And sexy black dots?
As an African American woman
I am constantly put on the spot

Tell me are you the mother of your earth?
Lying on your back to give birth?
Is it sometimes hard for you to smile?
Have you ever had to breastfeed
And raise another women's child?

Lady Bug, my ancestors been carrying the load
Of America in their belly's since the beginning of time
An African American woman's strength
Absolutely blows my mind.

Lady Bug, now let's get deep
Have you ever been raped, scorned, pimped or stoned?
Hung, chastised, criticized, dehumanized or terrorized?

No other woman in the history of this planet
Has gone through what my ancestors went through

Lady Bug, have you ever been disrespected?
Called out your name like a b*tch or ho*
To describe your assertiveness?
Do they think you are insane
For using your brain?

LADY BUG, as ladies can we just hang?
Is your world a better place for women of color?
Tell me lady bug, 'because I really need to know
If so, I am ready, willing and able to go

I saw a lady bug crawling on my wall today
And I said, "Hey, lady bug, you are alright with me!"

MISSING DAD

I never missed a thing
'Cause his presence was nonexistence
But still I went the distance
Afterschool programs, running track, talking smack
And eating my favorite snacks.

Too many missed moments to rewind and fulfill
Too many times when my allergies made me ill
But you cannot miss what you did not have
This is why I continue to smile, grin and laugh
I still went the distance and listened to my instincts

As a child running wild
I had the knowledge of my elders
Making sure I stayed covered
My big brothers and sisters still hold me down present day
God has blessed me with the ability to love even my haters
Which has safely guided me along the way

Indeed A father is a valuable tool, a guiding jewel for a girl
But God created me so I'm no fool
What I missed, I made up with time
Spent with UNC so much spunk
No punk, taking no punches but blessing
Our lives inspiring us to share, work harder and smarter

Uplifting and creating a new meaning and purpose
For all of the fatherless daughters, this is for you:
Stand strong, back straight, head held high
They help to create you
But you control your wings to FLY!!!
To your highest and greatest potential

THE CONVERSATION

Queen: "Hey, King"

King: "Hey, Queen. Lots been going on here in America"

Queen: "Shoot ain't nothing changed. Just a different form of
slavery and now they even control the weather, Can't sleep
anymore. Afraid to let my mind go free"

King: "Damn sis, afraid of what you might see? Black men,
women and children lying dead beside me. Not while
I'm around. I will hold you down, even if it takes them putting
me down"

Queen: "You do wear the crown but I see you frowning because
we are lost, some of us drowning in our own ignorance"

Both: "It was never meant for us to live as savages or slaves
Early arrivals to our graves
They keep talking about Black-on-Black crime

King: "More media lies but nice try"

Queen: All cultures and races commit crimes
Their focus on reporting people that look like you and I"

King: "But what about the woman that just killed her babies"

Queen: "Oh you mean Christy Sheats?
That Caucasian lady
Who ran her kids down
Shooting them dead in the street
While the father screamed for help in defeat"

King: "Wow, you on your shit deep"

Queen: "Got to be, a Black woman has the hardest job alive
Remember we been raped, pimped and scorned
Never forget we raised and breast fed white women's newborns
Let that marinate in the brain for a minute or two
So the hate for us runs deep"

King: "But ya'll wear it well in the streets
From your hair down to your feet
I just be wanting to hum, Hmm, hmm, hmm."

Queen: (Blushing). "Your sweet making me weak
Like the numbers 88, 311 and 4/20
Do people even know what that means?"
King: "Wait you going too deep"

Queen: "Please relax King, and let me speak
88 is the number for "Hail Hitler"
311 is the number for Ku Klux Klan
4/20 is Hitler's birthday
Too much murder happening now
And this just didn't begin"

King: "America has terrorized and killed people of all races and
cultures more than anyone else. If you want to know why a
group of people are reacting and acting out look at the slaves'
masters and read some real truth, then take a deep look in the
mirror and reflect"

Both: "'Cause they are deliberately killing us"

Queen: "Research your food and the ingredients within.
Watch what you eating: GMO's, pesticides and ramen noodles
poisoning our bodies. Dr. Sebi gave us knowledge to rise above
the disease of mucus. Everything else man-made enslaving
young minds to early graves. Unfocused ready to shoot or poke
something at will"

King: "Queen Stop! You giving me chills. You mean they
purposely making us ill?"

Queen: "Like chicken pox was the kill way back when, they
went way above and beyond killing generations of our families,
with the Tuskegee Experiment"

King: "Like we said"

Both: "It was never meant for us to live as savages or slaves,
early arrivals to our graves"

King: "Damn, Queen"

Queen: "Damn, King"

Both: "How can we not love one another? Look at the passion, compassion and knowledge we bring to each other"

THE GUN VS. THE KNIFE

The Gun: A weapon incorporating a metal tube from which bullets, shells or other missiles are propelled by explosive force, typically making a characteristically loud and sharp noise.

The Knife: An instrument composed of a blade fixed into a handle, used for cutting or as a weapon.

She was walking down the street
Returning from school to make dinner for her siblings

Cutting up the veggies, her brother runs into the kitchen
Five minutes later a knock at the door
Followed by a blast that didn't last long enough to save her

She was left dead gunshot to the head
How can you compare as we all look on and stared
The gun vs. the knife
It's time to fight back but how can you win
With bullets seeping into your skin
Filled with lead and poison

Will you be the next one chosen?
To feel the difference between the knife and the gun
See it's no fun
When the test is put to your child's chest
Face, back, neck, head, arm or leg
Cut or shot in any of these spots

Who will live? Who will die?
In critical condition they are conditioned to kill on sight
Those guns suddenly look like knifes
Wallets, soda bottles and potato chip bags
Are you seeing this **Sugar, Honey, Ice Tea?**

Chicago had the most homicides
468 in 2015 shot, tortured, stabbed killed dead?
But still we are filled with lies that divide people unequally
A White supremacy
Kind of inequality

So many lost and blinded
Poor Raven Simone
She thinks she's not Black
Making statements SHE believes to be true
There's a whole list of other lost Black African Americans
Are one of them you?

PUTTING PEN TO PAPER

I put the pen to the paper and so I write
I open my mouth but the words don't come out
So I look into the mirror to see if I like what I see
It's the history of a woman that has seen many things

Growing up in BK you have to live and look a certain way
It comes from the sway in your hips
The thickness of your thighs
The look they give you when they say, "Hi."

Who am I kidding when they say, "Yo baby, Yo baby, yo."
Back then you wasn't just called, "Hey, ho!"
Back then Black men hustled smarter for their doe
To feed their kids

Not stand in line for hours
To purchase the latest kicks

The pants were baggy but they didn't hang
All the way off their ass
Wearing dirty draws
Yo, for real that sh*t be making me mad

When my mom walked past
They offered to carry her bags
See back then we came outside to play
We wanted to see and hear our friends face-to-face
See what they had to say and who was coming out to play

Saw my first murder at the age of 14
See I never said the streets wasn't mean
But when the cops knocked at my door the next day
My mom proudly said, we absolutely have nothin' to say
It wasn't about snitching or making up a story for fame
Nowadays, if I don't like you and you have kids
I can call ACS, give your name, create a story
Making you and your children's lives a hot mess

I just want people to really wake up
And take the cold out their eyes
Observe what's in the mirror
And really see what's in the mirror
Reflect on something and someone good
Have we forgotten what it's like to be loved and respected?
Do you not see the changes happening around you?
Are we so caught up into ourselves
Fashion, celebrities and reality TV?

I put the pen to the paper and so I write
I open my mouth but the words don't come out
So I take a deep breath
Breathe easy and let the truth come out

WONDER WOMEN CREW

Adrianne, Asheba and me
Were the Wonder Women crew
Partying and shopping is what we liked to do
But don't get it twisted
Mess with us and we will beat your ass too

We were always ahead of our times
Been chilling with the original Wonder Women since '79
Her super human strength, animal cunning like moves
And sexy style is what made her cool

She taught us about the ideals of love, peace
And sexual equality
In a world torn by the hatred of men
A girl we knew in our neighborhood was raped
At the age of Ten
I often wondered where Wonder Woman was then

To stay focused and out of trouble
In our hood was challenging from the start
We went to school, played sports, worked
To help take care of our family

When people saw us coming they would say
"There go those Wonder Women girls again! Hey!"
Okay, I'll admit we had a drink or two
'Cause Wonder Women knows how to let her hair down too

Men would flock to us from left and right
Each of us had our own style that was out of sight
A guy grabbed Adrianne's buttocks in the club one day
And in the name of Wonder Woman, I quickly responded to say,

"You obviously have little regard for womanhood,
You will learn to respect us as women"
And we finished him off with a one-two that day

Our parents worked long hours to make ends meet
We were blessed to have a super hero
Who helped build our self-esteem and kept us on our feet
It's sad that there aren't any superhero women
To look up to today

So with these words from Wonder Woman,
I just want to say
A new journey to be started
It's time to make a new
The young is taking over
It's your turn to improve

Where we lacked, slacked and made mistakes
Keep God, love and family
A promise fulfilled and done with grace

Gracefully a new page to be written
Go forth unto this world with a pen in hand
Phone in the other, the paper awaits
Be adventurous, be creative and be original
Do YOU!!!

Above all else, be young
For youth is your greatest weapon
It's your greatest tool…use it wisely

WE ♥ EAST NEW YORK
WeLoveENY.org
positive images
+ positive examples
= success beyond measures
MENTORSHIP HELPS GROW OUR YOUTH

YOUNG SISTERS & QUEENS

Ethan Allen P.S. 306

This might be one of the hardest things I've ever had to write
The love I share for ya'll, no paper or pen can fulfill my plight
From the first day in Mrs. Glover's class
Extended Learning was the label
But we built a bond thicker after going through the stages of
Cain and Abel

God only knows how we got here
Family care giving, *Man Up, Inc.* was a part of the connection
Mrs. Chisholm and Mrs. Fung made the selection
For you to be here with me on Tuesday thru Friday at 2:15 pm
The more we indulge, the more we research and explore
The who, what, when, where, why and how
Self and cultural awareness, high school choices,
Conflict resolution, poetry, public speaking, health
Consciousness, life skills - we're doing it all

Staying LIT learning while having fun
Learning while having to tell Sis. Jada, Jayla, Kyla, and
Maniya to sit down and be quiet
While Sis. Charlenyes, Amirah, Gleneidy, Denise and both
Shade's are never disruptive, nor defiant

Sitting quietly ready to learn
Don't worry Sis. Perla, Yulana, and Ashley
I always feel the love and appreciate the love shown
Even when the Sista's
Roll their eyes and say, "Oh, my God!"

Trust me I get it.
I am you and you are me
Let us continue to learn how to bring out the positivity

And good attributes you possess so well
Don't keep them buried or hidden away in a shell

I see great potential in each and every one of you
Trust and believe I'll be here for you
Just remember not to stand in your own way
Continue to respect your elders
Listen to their wisdom 'cause it's priceless today
Don't believe what "They Say"
Make sure you research and do your own investigating
Along the way

Love conquers hate
Channel the negative people and energy away from you
You have too much to accomplish
Don't let a person, place or process stop nor distract you

You give me strength and helped me through
the toughest time in my life
My uncle's death, mother stricken with cancer
You helped uplift me to fight
For another day
To show up for work ready to see your faces
Discuss your future goals
While encouraging you to travel places

See the world meet different cultures
After all you are the original Queens
It will be their honor
So keep your head held high to the sky
Striving for the best
You are my first sisters' group
I am absolutely blessed

ANGELIC POETS

The following poems are written by group of young sisters known as the **Angelic Poets**, a group of young energetic sisters and "Brooklyn-nites" who attend Ethan Allen Middle School in Brooklyn, New York. Karen has mentored the Angelic Poets for the past two years. It was important for her to give these young poets a voice and to provide an opportunity for them to share their innermost thoughts and passions with all of you.

"GRANDMA" BY SHADE ELAM

You are my heart and my soul
You complete me through the cold
You love me and I love you
Let your story be told
Or let your PEACE hold

"BOOM" BY SHADE ELAM

Living in the neighborhood
Where all I hear is
Boom Boom Boom!!!!!!

It's not fair what a ten year old has to hear
Why do we choose violence?
Violence is not the answer

We should talk and listen to each other
Violence to me is like slavery
It's just not for us

Young ones to hear
Boom Boom Boom!!!!!
It's like hell bouncing in my soul

"REALLY?" BY MANIYA HENRY

Really?
Do we really need all these bad things happening in our city?
Every day I hear something bad happening on TV,
  the radio and in newspapers
Sometimes, I just ask myself do we really need
  all this negativity
My energy is in fear of everything now,
  even the ones that protect us
Everything that is happening is either stupid or unhealthy
And Lots of people agree with me.
There won't be one day when nothing's going wrong.
REALLY?

"BLOOM" BY MANIYA HENRY

Bloom like you were supposed to
I believe in you
So just bloom
You are so beautiful
And everyone loves you
Especially me,
And you know that
You are my best friend and sister
So just bloom into a beautiful flower
And I'll be your sister
Forever
So just bloom

"LOVE" BY MANIYA HENRY

Love, what is love
Love is when you care about someone
Love is when you give and don't take
Love is your family
Love is everything and everyone
Love is your friends
Love is your pets
The only question is how do you show it?
How do I love my family and my friends?

"DON'T JUDGE" BY MANIYA HENRY

Don't judge a book by its cover
If you do, you can hurt their feelings
You do not know who or how they really are
Sometimes when you do it to people
People will do it to you
That is why there is a popular saying
Don't Judge
A book by its cover

"WHY?" BY MANIYA HENRY

Why? Why did you have to leave me here hanging?
You were my only BFF
I felt like you didn't like me anymore
Because you stopped calling
I LOVE YOU

You are like a sister to me
Why did you leave me? Why?
We had the best sleepover ever

But then you just left
Without even saying goodbye
My only question is why?

"I BELIEVE" BY MANIYA HENRY

When I look at myself in the mirror
I see nothing but beauty
People say I am not worth it
That I am not beautiful
But I Believe

When I doubt myself
I say that I am confident
Because I Believe

When I look in the mirror at myself
I see my mom and say:
"I am Brave"
"I am Beautiful"
"I am Confident"

I Believe
I Believe
I Believe
I am Mainya Henry,
Sincerely to myself

"YOU" BY AMIRAH RIDDICK

You complete me
You bring me joy and happiness
How would I live without you?
I'm not really sure

Thinking of a time that I could lose you
Brings my heart cold and my eyes teary
How could I not thank you enough?

You are the one who got me on top and
Made me your twin
It's not hard to say
I love you, for what you did
Now let's take time to go through

You gave me the honor roll
You gave me hope to succeed to the next grade
You helped me accomplish the hardest
My pageant was all you

Last but not least
Principal's honor roll
For the first marking period in fifth grade

As you can see you are pretty awesome
Some might say, "Ugh! I hate my mom."
But You
You are a keeper!

"ROYALS" BY AMIRAH RIDDICK

We are all royals
From the crowns on our heads
To the heels on our feet

Show your royal colors
Let your inner you shine
Only you matter
FOR YOU ARE DIVINE

Hold your head high
Make dreams in your head
While you lay in your bed
Hold your dress with passion

Walk down your runway with pride
For You Are Divine
You are divine
You are divine
Let your inner power shine

Grow up young royals
Bring happiness to the world
But always remember
YOU ARE THE ONE

And others gonna hate
Better concentrate
Because dreams don't come easy
It's them you have to chase

"COLOR" BY AMIRAH RIDDICK

I see color
The color of Love
The color of Courage
The color of a Nation
The color of Forces Mixing

Hand-in-hand
One-on-one
Together we can make memories of love
Slavery shall not be done
We must stick together as one
No more cops or shootings
Just give a hug or a symbol of love

In Our Hearts
It Beats For the Love
Of Different Colored People and such

It's not the way you dress or look
It's the way you carry yourself
People can't see what's inside of you or me
The colored and discolored must love with their hearts
Not our heads
Together As One
That means color is no match for love

"UNTOLD STORIES" BY AMIRAH RIDDICK

Untold stories, unknown but never forgotten
Tales told within our skin color
Letting us know we still matter
Heart turn to pieces by the blade called life
Our ancestors did more than become slave and owned

We built this Nation
A nation that is treated different than the suburbs
But then again that's another untold story

Hidden in our hearts deep within
But we are taught to love other people, but they can love us too
Not knowing when to pull out our untold stories
Thinking that we will be laughed at and judged

Some stories rut in mold never making it out to the surface
But we are people too
And we have so much more to say than "he's dead"
We can write and speak our minds
But most of all
We can tell those untold stories hidden deep within

Our skin is what makes us
It's why we have so many untold stories
So love yourself
If you feel you're not wanted make yourself feel wanted
You don't need anyone else to tell you
What to wear or what to do
Because you are another untold story
Waiting to be told to our youth

"BLACK GIRL" BY AMIRAH RIDDICK

Black Girl, hold your head high
Black Girl, touch the sky
Black Girl, times are rough
Black Girl, you're enough

Take your time, do not rush
All time is in your hands
Hold your crown sit up tight

Wish on stars that you see tonight
Then you will wake up better than great
A Kings life's success on one big plate
You should stand up straight

Hold your dress, fix your shoes only quitters lose
But you black girl, you have strength
You Congratulation and Accommodate the needs of others

"BEST FRIEND" BY KYLA GASKIN

Best friends know best
When thinking of my best friend
I know she will be there for me
Even if I'm not there for myself

Who will cheer me to my greatest heights?
Who will console me when I've fallen down?

She will stand up for me and lie down beside me
She will forgive me when I've hurt her and even bite her tongue
She could have easily said, "I told you so."

"LOVE" BY KYLA GASKIN

I Need Your Love
You said goodbye
And I thought I would die
I wanted to cry

Maybe you will see through my tears
I gave it one more try
It hurt as I cried

I tried to smile but I failed
I don't want to beg for your love
Nor ask for your sympathy

If you loved me, you would stay
Even when I'm pushing you away

"I NEED YOU" BY KYLA GASKIN

Because you are thought about in such a special way
Because you do so much to brighten people up day by day
Because you cared for others your whole life through
I say a little prayer each day especially for you

That heaven will protect you
And let you know
You meant so much to me

As I travel on life's way
And will keep you in my heart forever
Each and everyday

"I MISS YOU" BY KYLA GASKIN

I miss you more than I thought I would
And I cried much more than I thought I could

Time heals all
That's what they say
But love is the price and so I pay

Sometimes I smile
And I know you hear
It's not enough

Because you are not there
The years roll by
And I am not the same
Yet in my heart you still remain

You left Love behind
When you flew away
And I still love you to this day

"BECAUSE YOU CALL ME A FRIEND"
BY KYLA GASKIN

Because you call me a friend
I will give you a hug anytime

Because you call me a friend
I will hold your hand when you need it

Because you call me a friend
I will wipe away the tears when you cry

Because you call me a friend
I will listen when nobody else will

Because you call me a friend
I will not judge you

Because you call me a friend
I will forgive you
When you are mean to me

Because you call me a friend
You are a crutch when I cannot walk
My eyes when I cannot see through the blurriness
And my ears when I cannot hear the truth
That is why I am you friend and you are mine

"YOU TELL ME" BY KYLA GASKIN

You tell me that you love me
You tell me that you won't leave
But you turn around and do it any way
I am crying my heart out
Hoping you hear me

But you ignore my painful cry
As each and every day passes by

I fake a smile to the world
But underneath there is no smile

Just my broken heart
The only good memories you gave me?

Is the thing I have left of you
Beginning to slowly fade away?

As time goes by
I am wondering everyday
Will I get over you?

"NEVER" BY KYLA GASKIN

Never say I love you if you really don't care
Never talk about feelings if they aren't really there
Never hold my hand if your gonna break my heart
Never say you are going to if you don't plan to start
Never look into my eyes if all you do is lie
Never say HI if you really mean goodbye
If you really mean forever then say you will try
Never say forever cause forever makes me cry

"EAST NEW YORK" BY SADE MALLOY

Wow I can't live in a place
Where I hear gunshots, fighting, plus more

I don't want my four year old cousin
Asking what is that BOOM sound
It hurts my heart to know that me and my four year old cousin
Knows exactly what that sounds like

I feel that's very bad
And it makes me sad and mad sometimes
But I choose to stay strong
Because gunshots tear families apart
And bring other lives to shame
It's just wrong!

"GRANDMA" BY SADE MALLOY

My Grandma is my life
She is my backbone, air and eyes
I love her

When God took my Grandma
My soul turned cold
I know she knows
She's my one and only Grams

I love you, hope to see you soon
I was her first grand
Love: Aw, Beep-Beep

Child when she had a heart attack
My dad said, "You going to have a grandchild!"
She lived eleven more years

Those eleven more years were not enough
I love and miss her
My heart is gone
Kisses up above

"DONALD TRUMP" BY SADE MALLOY

Wow, Donald Trump became President
Pain in a lot of people's souls
Joy in the hearts of others

Black brothers and sisters hoping
Trump won't make life worse
Afraid Trump will break Obama Care
Afraid blacks and whites won't get along

Has anyone thought about
How we all can work together?
Without all the panic
Doing what we can?
The world is coming to an end
Without anyone realizing it

Believe it or not
There is nothing wrong with people who like Trump
But we can't let Trump damage us
Or prevent us from helping other
brothers and sisters to live

51

"THE BROKEN HEART"
BY GLENEIDY HERNANDEZ

I never loved anyone as I love you, my dear
Since you left me my days are not the same
And my night is gloomy

It is because of you that my life seems lost in the tide
My days are not the same, my love
I truly adored you from the heart
From the start

Then why did you leave me alone
Life looks like a stone
Without emotions of the heart

I promised myself that I would not cry
Broken hearts don't easily mend
It's tough but I'm trying to get used to it
Hope you are doing fine

52

ULEA BARNES

The following lyric was written by Ulea Barnes, a high school student of Karen's who was courageous enough to step outside her comfort zone to broaden her horizons.

ᏏᎳᏍᏉ

MIRROR

In a video, my black brother Dwayne said,
"If you look into a mirror, you can see your soul"

I am wondering, if I sneak a glance into my soul
Which one of my secrets would be told?
People swear they know me
But how true can that be
When I don't really know myself

So quick to judge and point a finger
I done seen stuff that half of ya'll can't even dream of
I try every day to act like it don't affect me
Especially the ones who keep trying to test me

I mean, was there ever a moment when you felt alone?
Where you would just sit and question your life's role?

What happen to all the people who said they'd be there for me?
Where were they when I needed them most
While I was killing myself mentally?

Suck it up, Lea, and put your brave face on
Do what you got to do to keep yourself sane
There are things people don't know about you
Like the monsters who keep coming for you

I pray to God that things get better
"Father Can you hear me?"
I need you to help me make it through the day
I'm afraid okay? But I don't want anyone to know
Because if I don't play the game right
They will use my emotions for their own personal show

LENA SOUL

The following literature was written by a colleague and true friend of Karen's, who joined the task of mentoring the sisters group in 2016, to collectively and poetically develop creative young minds.

CONFIDENCE

They say, "Dress to impress" but I say,
"Don't forget to let the inner you Show
up to that interview!"
That position is yours

Just as long as you pause
Take a deep breath and accept your flaws
As bookmarks to the many chapters of your life
To remind you of the many times you had to fight
And no one knew
But in those times you grew internally
Affecting your ability to express yourself verbally

You heard of me
They call me confidence
I reside somewhere in the depth of your consciousness
Longing to appear on your chest
But instead I'm buried back here behind
The memories of your incompetence
The one's right next to cluttered stacks of self-doubt
I'm trying hard not to shout
But you've stored a lot of things between me
And that path from your brain to your mouth

So no one sees or hears how
I'm trying to represent you with smile
Like Cochran did at OJ's trial
But I can't get past this huge stockpile
Of memories of when you were ridiculed as a child.
It's time to throw these away!
I've tripped on them twice today
Trying to catch up to the words
You were just about to say
But a bag of insecurity

Beat me to your lips
So I sit way back here in the grips
Of the web of negativity that has formed
In the back of your mind
Where I'm behind
Multiple file cabinets that are
Holding your vile habits
And every bad thing that's ever happened to you
Since you were two years of age

It's time to throw these away
So what you're gay?
So what you were a prostitute?
So what you've been to jail?
So what they're all doubting you?
And so what the rumors that are circulating are true?
So What?!
Get rid of everything!

Like Spring cleaning
Start with some self-seeking
Keep only the things that don't remind you of hell
leaking Into your new space
Allow me to move with grace
On a clear path through your mind
Allow me to fill your spine
And reassemble your posture
Stand tall and walk in
But not as an imposter

Only as the perfectly imperfect being that you are
with me, confidence, they'll see a blazing star
You may be dressed to impress but unless
You let that new 'inner you' show up to that
interview You're just another attractive mess
Claiming to be the best
Without confidence

KAREN YELVERTON

The following poems are by Karen Yelverton honoring all the ordinary and yet extraordinary people who extended a helping hand while she was facing difficult times on land.

Every mistake and challenge is a lesson learned.

WHAT WOULD YOU DO?

To Nadia and All Those Who Choose To Do Right

What would you do?
What's wrong or right?
Step in, help out, break up the fight
Or on site, take flight, hit record and zoom in real tight
While the guy hits the girl
'Cause in his world and on the "tell-a-lie" vision
He sees a chump—I mean Cheetos, I mean Trump
Saying, "Just grab 'em by the pus**"

Would you be strong enough to stand up?
For the girl who only knows what she's been told
Since five years old that a woman's
Only good for cooking and cleaning
By eleven she's good enough to lay on her back
While bending over with a big rack
Twerking required, otherwise she's considered wack

Or would you be willing to reach out to her
Teach her, show her, talk to her, listen to her?

Or would you do what's wrong?
String her along, buy her new shoes, clothing and jewels
Or maybe sing her favorite song which will surely have a line like
"Bit*h don't snitch…you know you want this di*k"

Would you do what's right?
Step in, break up a fight, or on site take flight
Hit record and zoom in real tight
While the girl smacks the guy
'Cause she's too fly to get played
After being named "wifey" with a third baby on the way

She says it's over, SMACK, SMACK!
Then calls her "Cuzzo"
Always strapped, takes no slack
Says he'll finish him, CLAP, CLAP!
One to the head the other through the
chest Came out his back, all caught on live

'Cause Some would rather hit record and ignore
Promoting being a coward sucker ass dude
It's harder nowadays to think things through to move smarter
Our morals and values worthless, why bother

Because I know a girl named Nadia
Who is smarter than most adults
I knew in their teens
Poised, educated and patient,
You wouldn't even believe

And yes, she did what was right on site
When on site she could have reacted making a difference choice
Another chapter of a show being recorded
Displaying the patience of an angel at that age
With impeccable stamina and strength

Eighty percent certain she helped save a young boy's life
'Cause on site she chose an option not as popular these days
To take a stand and do what was right

I am a teaching artist because of Queen Nadia
A sister like her I will always fight for and write
She listened to her mother's parenting skills and her BFF's
How important it is to surround yourself with nothing or no one short
Of being and giving their very BEST

LENA 100 YEARS YOUNG

September 26, 2016

You are truly blessed
You have lived 100 years
It's not every day somebody turns a century

You have lived 10 decades
Ten decades of memories, experiences, happiness
And changes to say the least

You are a living legend
A queen with the Spirit guiding you
Your strength has shown us the will to live life
To love and forgive, even when things don't add
up Or when people and things are not always fair

Never let life's struggle take control or
interfere Never give up or show fear
No road to success is easy
No one man or woman can do it alone

But today we are blessed to be in your presence
Heavenly sent as mother earth
You represent so much more as we gather
To celebrate 100 years on this your born day

May you be blessed to see many more
You go "beauty queen," it's your time
Celebrate and give thanks for you are Divine

For this moment cannot be taken for granted
We look to your inspiration and strength
Thanks for sharing your day with F.D.A
Frederick Douglas Academy VI

THE THRILL FROM THE HILL
THAT FILLS MY SOUL

Dedicated to the Legacy of Mrs. Judy Sturgis Hill

The thrill from the hill that fills my soul:
Once a judge, Judy never seems to grow old

With her "Sturgis" smile
She can stop for a while
Just to say "howdy" or "hello"
Always so jolly just like Jell-O
But oh so mellow inside

Like music from a Chello
A voice so mild
A champion of women
Brains and beauty came with you
From Nights of Pithest to EMU.

The who, what, where and why
You reached us when you taught us
Made us really truly try

Now I am glad that I listened
And glistened in the spotlight
You taught me how to win
And compete without a fright

We are sure what you stand for
Shines brightly on your face
One space, one place, one human race
Only the pure can endure

Life's hustle and haste, why waste time to hate
When you can do it with love

Let faith be your mate
On the wings of a dove

Feel this thrill from the hill, let it kill this cold
Mrs. Judy you are hotter than melting gold
So precious and priceless like a diva with a plan
Reach out to touch somebody's hand
Yes, you made this world a better place
Now we can
Do not let a person, place or process steal your joy
Your words are for great men, women, girls and boys

So when I am in a place of real adversity
And this campus feels like calamity
I battle my blows with your bravado words
Hold my head up, big smile on my face
And bitterness turns into the Manuka Honey that I taste

The true EMU you knew was like family
With connections for all
Like you meeting Kirk and a wife for Paul
Michael was lucky he met his dear wife here
But when Pat went to marry, she did so elsewhere

On this day that is dedicated to a great Black dreamer
We ask our Lord, our God and our Blessed Redeemer
For showers of blessings for you tonight
To honor you for all the things you did so right

From recruiting Uncle Ray to working with Dennis B
To winning oratory down in Washington, DC
With your dear late friend, DeAnthony JB
Now that he is resting so very heavenly

You pray and always say, "Don't judge a book by its cover"
Watch the clock when they block, just move on over
Find a way just to say, "Love your brother and sister"

Hi fives, hugs and holla, say hello to the fellow
Find a tribe just to vibe
But whatever your do, keep hope alive

Once upon a time, just a few years ago
Before there was Facebook and Twitter, you know
Ms. Judy and her friends met face-to-face
No Instagram, no selfies, no cell phones to replace

Real people, real smiles, real exquisite taste
Real friends, real family, real fans in this place
Real hands, real arms, real warm embrace
"I got to get my hugs," she said to your face

Still, this thrill from the hill can fill all our souls
Look right, look left, there are persons to hold
That patented Judy hug she planted deep in us
Though we fight at night and some days we fuss
There is always someone who deserves our trust

Your "Sturgis" style from a child says to fight that fear
Yes, we love you Mrs. Judy,
You are a treasure, we celebrate your legacy my dear

JULIA LINGOES

My sister, my friend
The one who always opened up her home to let me in
As we smile laugh out loud and grin
Your kindness was birthed from a child
A loving giving spirit always true and free
I'm lucky and blessed to have you indeed
My sister, my friend from NYC to Michigan
Julia Lingoes I love you

MIKE MARION

Mike Marion the man
With the Persuasion, POI and DUO plan
Always prepared to take life on with a storm
Making sure he does no harm.
Rhetorically, he'll rock your world
Even fell in love with a beautiful Asian girl

You see Mike Marion is a smooth brother
That's right, my brother from another mother
He's helped many of us reach beyond the stars
Making sure we are educated and always looking good by far

His love for cats is for real
Mess With one in front of him and its kill, kill, kill
His heart is big along with his passion to help others is strong
We will miss you Mike Marion
EMU and Forensics will forever be your home

In a world full of racism, evil and hate
You found a way to coach my heart with no barriers or color lines
Giving me a few tools to shake off the haters
While making each and every performance great

LAURIE WALKER

Laurie, Laurie where have you been?
It's been a while since I've seen your beautiful
face I made it back safely to the EMU in one place.
One degree completed and a master's on the way
Happy, healthy and blessed for another day

Working to change negative perceptions
Of women and African Americans along the way
Remembering being recruited in California by Uncle Ray
Who knew what changes were headed my way

Mentors like Dr. Doris, Mrs. Judy Sturgis Hill
and Laurie (you too)
Helped inspire me to work harder
And want even more out of life
Thanks for helping me understand the importance
Of my educational plight

SURGEONS

The Dedicated Surgeons Who Performed
Mother's Cancer Surgery

Surgeons are among some of the most highly educated
And well paid professions in the U.S.A.
But to the Yelverton's it means so much more
Displaying a caring personality wanting to explore

Fixing human beings without even seeing the future
But taking it into your own hands
Reading 1,000's of test results
Only someone shadowing you and your team
Would understand

The debt, tenacity, conscious training
You bring to each operation
Comforting families without hesitation
Clarifying realistic resolutions
Displaying emotional empathy

Thanks for choosing such a highly profound profession
And for every moment you spent
Removing my mother's cancerous cells
Let's not forget about your Dream Team from
Danielle To Rita, the Nurses, Anesthesiologist
And the New York University staff
Your professionalism, patience, communication
Was first class

With so many operations under your belt
It's probably work as usual
But for this poet every operation is a miraculous touch
With spiritual interludes

Thank you Dr. Newman
Your name alone tells me that you give people
A new chance at living healthy
Dr. Newman = A new woman and new man

SISTER DOMINQUE YATES

One of the Greats
A queen with a style meaningful and unexplainable
Following in your Father's footsteps
You are the best at what you do

Keep your head held high
Staying true to your roots

Uplifting your ancestors every chance that you get
Without regret
Focusing on making the best
Out of every day in everyway

You are the glue that holds things together
Hotep man up, sister love forever
I got your back no matter what the weather
Rain, sun, snow, thunder, no need to wonder
You're up next Wonder Woman
Let them feel your thunder

BUDDHA

Most high King Wizard of the streets
How you defeated the odds
By hanging with mobsters to switching up providing them with
legal jobs
To uplifting the community with a common unity
To Man Up Stand Up for what is right

Finding a new meaning to fight back
Making a difference through singing, laughter and too many jokes
But when the smoke clears
You're standing tall by our side with no fear

Not known to show the sensitive side
But from me your Lil Sis, you cannot deny or hide
The love we share since I was knee high
Daring to dream of being the best at whatever I do
Because I looked up to people like you
Aka "Bugski", my big brother, I love you too

SISTER EBONY DAVIS

Sister Ebony Davis
Earth day October 2
Six years with the Organization

After school and summer school
Office Manager and Assistant to Brother P
Must have been the hardest job, if you ask me

Mini stalker who never wants her to leave
She's irreplaceable you see
aka Miss Nice-Nasty, Professional and Classy
Beware you might catch her on a bad day
How can you tell? Look at them eyes and her face

But if it's Sister Rhonda, Marisol, Dom or me
Pleeeeeeeease, we just look and laugh while we hum a
Keisha Cole song
Thanks for your tenacity and the need to get things done right
You have helped us all especially when the candy jar was in site
Always willing to go the extra mile
With a little "tude" to remind you
That "No, I'm not rude, just not in the mood for your BS excuses"
Or long drawn out story of no good news

In the words of Oprah,
"I don't think of myself as a poor deprived ghetto girl who made good.
I think of myself as somebody who, from an early age,
knew I was responsible for myself, and I had to make good."
(Economy, 2015)

She's off to her next journey as you will be truly missed
We salute you Sis cause you're the twin of my best friend
Plus my mother loves you and thinks you're the sweetest.

BROTHER A.T. MITCHELL

STEP BY STEP, WE SAY "HOTEP"

'Cause lean streets are mean streets for
Hungry youths weaning off the milk of motherhood
Misunderstood by the masses, skipping classes
Like an express train, racing aimlessly to the final pain
Of spent lead…dead
But you do not give up, making them live up
To the Man Up, you create to abate
The flow of bad vices like dope
Mad devices kill hope
And stifle dreams with screams of fear
As young hearts beat their last red rhythm
Voiceless victims
Of a violent system

STEP BY STEP, WE SAY "HOTEP"

'Cause you see raw talent in the rejected sisters or brothers
Outside the norm respected for brains like rain drops in a storm
Dropping great ideas by the buckets,
Popping eyes straight out their sockets
But stopped in stride by empty pockets
What? "Not now, I ain't got it yet" but somehow you still allotted it
No complaints for man up miracles,
Painting pride like shiny spectacles
On faces smiling to say "Thank You"

STEP BY STEP, WE SAY "HOTEP"

'Cause you get that rep for pep talking
Prepping us for walking into a brand new building
797…Oh, what a feeling
Of fine floors like good hood heaven with photo decors

That say pause, look at me, please
Reflections of man up visionaries
You trained to tease youthful senses
Removing stress and mental fences
Turning success from past offenses

Well, well, Bro Mitchell
So many stories you can tell
Block by block, making a community better
Tick by tock, your time saves yet another brother
Programs like JDC, Father Initiative, Don't Shoot NYC
Cure Violence…they all still live

Still, that unwritten will by the late little Deasean Hill
Inspires you to fill youths with lifelong skills
For on your earth day, you do the giving
So they can enjoy the thrill of living because
STEP BY STEP, WE SAY "HOTEP"

OSEI

A poet must write but before she can write
She must research so that every single word flows
Truthfully from the soul
In celebration of a Man of God:
    Husband, Father, Grandfather, Great Grandfather,
    Godfather,
    Uncle, Cousin, Mentor, Teacher, Coach and Friend

Osei defined as a great love for humanity
High ideals loves to help others
Love for life is important to him
Inclined to solitude, preferring to be alone
Than in bad company
Sis. Sharoyah your fate was set
And written this way for the both of you

To see life is nice, living it out on your own terms it's only right
That a celebration be given in your honor 65 years younger,
Teaching the youth to aim higher, keep reaching, try harder

Traveling the world, family, education, religion and health
Smarter than most your age walking this earth
Beside every good man is his queen, Sis. Sharoyah mother earth

Ancestry, generations you taught them first
How to get from behind yourself and stand up for what you believe
Conscious self-awareness if nothing else
We learn before we read or write
If you "Black Get Back," if you "Brown Stick Around,"
If you "Yellow You Mellow," and if you "White You Alright"

Well you flipped it
'Cause an intelligent King will never sit back
But obtain his crown helping the Black, Yellow and Brown
Stand ground
For future generations to not drown in ignorance

While the revolution will not be televised
Your positive influences help family and friends take pride
Knowing we will rule once again
You made it through decades of "Willie Lynching" tactics

Standing strong with your beliefs bringing you to this day
Take a moment look around, this is a part of God's blessings
Not one mistake was made or found
So continue living, loving life, safely
Appreciating your blessings each day
Lamar and I know you hit the lotto—where's our cut at anyway?

LISA DOZIER

Thanks to my friend Lisa
Whom I've known since a little girl
Brooklyn's version of Mother Teresa with a heart of pure gold
With your magical touch you mend and mold
Many minds and bodies to leave this old world
With comfort so soothing it heals all our souls
Friends, families or fans across all households

In this time of our grief, what a relief you are
Like that brightest star dashing across a dark sky
Just to tell us why life moves on
To that next light in the nearest dawn
After the dusk, when quiet nights in deep slumber sleep
Say hush, just to rush dreams of best times back into our hearts

Streaming teams of butterflies when champs depart
That float like little Ali's cross my memories
Or sting like busy bees with jabs of tears
Yet tickling my ears with warm waning whispers
Of voices that ease the pain when sadness simmers

Amidst all this, when sorrows persist against life's bliss
You dare to hug and kiss us
Never stare or dismiss us
Your smile cheers us to wish us well and live to tell
The greatness of our loved one, a champ gone to run
The best race he has already won beyond the golden sun

This is meant for you Lisa: daughter, mother,
sister, mentor and wife
Your strength makes it easier
To slice away our strife
Like a knife, sharpened by your own humanity and caring
On my soul I am wearing these words I am sharing

To thank angels like you who God selected for us
As the bravest, the few, to renew our trust
In life, love and living so dear
To pray away those fleeting fears
And wipe away those teasing tears
That chase each other down our cheeks
You make us strong for the comfort we seek

In this magical moment when the champ meets the Savior
May He bless you with His highest favor
And from all of us, the Yelverton family
And especially from me
May the good Lord make you touch, feel, taste, hear and see
Miracles, sweet showers of riches and business success
For it took a champion like YOU
To make our champ look the best

ADRIANNE

At the age of five she taught me to share
At Ernie's Pizzeria they showed us their love
$5.00 became $2.50 each for a slice, icy and cold drink
She went to PS 306 while I went to "Grace,"
A Baptist school and church that helped shape
The woman I am academically and spiritually

I was blessed with many sisters
Victorious blessings, we were sanctioned
I would have an early dismissal, changed into my
uniform To meet "A" up at the school

It was Junior High now, we knew we were breaking rules
People begin to test you, feeling themselves with new outfits
Somehow it gave them the courage to be rude
Calling you names, stepping on your new shoes

But not me and "A," we had a crew: Asehba, Kali, Chandra,
Thalia, Tamara, Meka Luv, Venus and Nicole to name a few
Each of us had our own style
Hanging out late, watching people running wild

Back when fighting and 52 hands touch was the style
Violence took place back then
However I never felt unsafe, living was a priority
The goons sent us upstairs
'Cause they were always looking to win
Whether running track or working at the grocery store packing bags
"A" and I shared many meals and laughs

I never realized how much I adore
The influence she has on me
Always ready to take on more of what life had in store
She implores
The beauty of a true dear sister, mentor, and friend

Rocking for over 30 years
Laughter, joy Heartache and tears
Words cannot match up or explain
Family, Sister, Coach, Mentor, Friend
With her there is no ending

SERENA WILLIAMS

Intelligent, beautiful and kind in all ways
Go-getter, trendsetter, reigning champion of Wimbledon
WTA Tour, French, Australian and U.S. Open
Pause
23 Grand Slams!

Never hesitating to take ball and racket in hand
As I accolade on then
Most singles, doubles and mixed doubles
Not that shi* you get from the bar
This mega super star can challenge her challenger
While remixing and dancing to "Bey" 7/11 7/11

Knowing God and her sister, Yetunde, are smiling down from heaven
Saying we got you sis, stay focused stay strong
Hit that racket to right every wrong
Born in Michigan raised in Compton
Parents, Richard and Oracene, did things their way

You and your sister Venus at the age of three,
Facing racism at National Junior Tournaments at ten
Which help build tough skin,
Shaking off ignorance with a smile since back then

None of us can walk a mile in your shoes
Your focus under pressure unspeakable
Proven to be unbeatable almost every time
Showing the world just how good
Natural Black Beauty, Class, Elegance, Intelligence and Talent look
All wrapped up in a Queen

Competing in a sport that was not always welcoming
Of women or people of color
But after the Williams sisters
A new era of power tennis was born

It's your time to shine on sistahs, shine on
Body banging, I repeat—BODY BANGING—no surgery needed here
Inspiring children of all colors worldwide

While they wait for the day to hit that ball to their next opponent
Reminiscing on every moment displayed
By The Greatest of all time
Serena Williams, aka The "GOAT"

ATTENTION! ATTENTION!

Train riders listen up, there are rules to follow
So, please take note of this announcement
BE QUIET and HUSH UP:

FIRST, buy your metro card in advance
It will give you and everyone else a chance
At a good ride, so swipe and keep things moving along

SECOND, when the train stops, allow people to get off first
How hard is that, damn it
It's crowded enough without having to dodge
Between passengers trying to get off
Just stop and move aside until all the passengers are off
Besides, conductors only keep the doors open long enough
To sneeze, not breathe

THIRD, when entering the train, move all the way in
There is so much more room hidden on the inside for you
And my ladies with big twins to
Making the ride more comfortable
With less people rubbing against you
While perverts trying to hump you

FOURTH, give up your seat for the elderly, disabled, pregnant
or those in need Some conductors are so rude and impatient
With the elderly quick to close those doors and leave
Just hold the door open and do your job

You can be late coming into the station and that is a fact
Guess you didn't know I knew that, this simple deed and act
In extending kindness towards humanity on display
For you never know what challenges
You may encounter along the way

FIFTH, cover your mouth when you cough or sneeze
No one wants to inhale your sickness
or God forbid, any other particles flying out your mouth
Too many unknown incurable diseases

SIXTH, don't squeeze into places where you damn well
know you can't fit
What kind of mess is that?
You mad cause they slim and you fat?

SEVENTH, buy some headphones
No one wants to hear that garbage you are playing
To each is own…tomatoes, tomato's

EIGHTH, no random filming or picture taking
of people you don't know
Stop making fun of people exposing them by recording them,
stick to selfies, film yourself yolo solo

NINTH, if you're not sure, don't give out incorrect directions
Telling folks, "I don't know" works a lot better than getting them lost

TENTH, be kind and smile at fellow passengers
People are always going through something
Your life is sustainable you survive as a transit passenger

FUSION

FUSION – The scientific process that merges atoms together to create energy. Fusion cuisine is cuisine that combines the elements of at least two different styles of cooking.

F   Fascinate
U   Unification
S   Soulful
I   Innovation
O   Optimistic
N   Nurturing

Thanking each and every one of you,
From the left to right and front to back.
Let's make this event LIT
Standing out from the rest
With some of the best
Artists and talents to come through this town
In Brooklyn, we have been known to shut sh*t down

So it's only right
That we take flight
On the journey of poetry and spoken word
In our Neighbor-Hood
There is common unity
Speaking from the heart to our community

TV, radio and social media
All share lies about what they want you to hear
Rest in peace, Orlando victims, I swear
But they forgot to mention the deadly floods in Ghana
Were people are dying and coming up missing
Oh, and they are Black like you and I,
Just in case I forgot to mention

But the murdering didn't start there
And it sure wasn't the largest or deadliest
Mass terrorist massacre in U.S. history
So let's break down "His-Story"

1917 East St Lois Massacre: 200-700 deaths
1919 Arkansas Massacre: 854 deaths
1921 Tulsa Massacre: 300-3000 deaths
1923 Rosewood Massacre: 150 deaths

And that's just to name a few
Of how they screw with the human brain
Playing mind games to gain fame
Leaving the hard working people slain and stained with untruths
Falsities that lead our people to fatalities against each other

As I sit and watch, So You Think You Can Dance
They steal all our moves but tell us we can't move forward
In all the things that we first started
Man, these devils been cold hearted
Since their birth
So, we must become the change we all want to see
And you won't find it on
Empire, Snap Chat, Facebook or ratchet TV

But my God, your presence here tonight
has already made a change and sacrifice
Supporting the arts, artists and black owned business
The "East" will never be the same, for we have gathered
to be ordained, proclaiming victory and greatness

OUR FATHER

Our Father, full of grace, bless this boy
    With his magnificent face

Bless his hair that is a little bald
    Keeping him just for me that's all

Bless him that he is big and strong
    Teach him how to keep his hands where they belong

Bless him in the future so he understands
    I am his woman and he is my man

Bless his parents day and night
    Because of them, he is such a beautiful sight

Bless his eyes that shine like stars
    And may he like me most of all

Bless the big, bless the small
    Bless his heart most of all

Bless his body that always sweats
    When playing basketball at his best

Bless his tongue that taste Divine
    And may it stay on top of mine

Bless our plans for forever and ever
    But most of all, keep us together

Bless my feelings that are ever so strong
    That he will never do me wrong

LOVE

Love is a game you don't play to win
You play to survive

Through good and bad times
We shall be together to weather any storm
So never give up or in to love
Make it survive

Denying it can and will hurt your pride
Unable to condition yourself
For the next level of loving
Missing out on what's meant for you bugging

Unable to think, eat or sleep
The devil comes in all shapes and sizes
With hatred running deep

You feel it when you walk into the room
Love them back even though they don't love themselves
Winning tool

BAG LADIES

B	Beautiful	**L**	Loving
A	Amazing	**A**	Admirable
G	Graceful	**D**	Delightful
		I	Impeccable
		E	Educated
		S	Sister from the East side

Women of color, in color working for the people
Seeing and bringing out the best in each woman that crosses our path

Never getting our just due credit so we just smile and laugh
Staying humbled to the cause of accolades and rewards
That come from up under

Our young queens
Who dare to dream
Of womanhood
Wanting theirs to change way before their time
Trust us young queens
Stay young and enjoy your youthful years
Take your time 'cause when it's time,
You will have your work cut out for you

See, we always hold our people down
Original creators of the "Black Lives Matter" movement
Yes, it all starts with you—all of you

Let's have a moment of silence
"Sandra Bland", we will never forget you

So, never hesitate to be great
We are living and speaking for those
Who have been falsely accused, murdered and raped

We are the chosen ones
They already knew we were great
Pardon me,
I mean the greatest at whatever we put our minds to do
There is nothing wrong with loving your people
So long as you are conscious first and loving you

AMERICA: "A MURDEROUS PLACE TO LIVE"

AMERICA: "A MURDEROUS PLACE TO LIVE"
Where we have been systematically programmed from the
start And have passed it along to our kids
Now we have a long history of abusing people,
The environment, and the political system
So my brothers and sisters I ask you WHY?

Why are we so surprised?
At the rise of crime that has kept us high
On our Willie Lynching ways that have kept us
Enslaved to this day
Thots "twerking" and "lurking" for butt shots
Filled with poison that can kill you on the spot
Oh, she thinks she is hot "NOT"

When Sarah Baartman's beautiful full-figured body
Was put on display
For their amusement in a disgraceful way
Due to their racist brutality for 1,461 days
That still exists to this day
Do you know who you really are?

Black women are legendary pioneers in this game
But their history has tried to erase them from our brains
Leaving an unknown stain of ignorance
Filled with Christopher Columbus and Harry Potter lies

Stripped of their contributions and identification Zora Neale
Hurston, Bell Hooks, Francis Crest, Alice Walker, Nikki
Giovanni, Sister Souljah
And the miraculous cells of Henrietta Lacks,
Whose cells were stolen by doctors in 1951 to analyze
And SURPRISE! Her cells are still alive today

Helping to develop the polio vaccine
And assisting in cancer research and AIDS
Meanwhile, there was no family compensation
While her cells were spread all across America's murderous nation,
For the purpose of gentrification.
Not sure if they shared that with you in your text book "His-Story"
Excuse me but these Black Queens
Are the Marilyn Monroe's that inspired me

AMERICA: "A MURDEROUS PLACE TO LIVE"

A place that pretends to give a fu**
As long as you have enough bucks, cash, grass or selling your ass
So while teaching class, I had to ask,
"What are your future goals in life?"
One student replied, "A basketball player!"
Another said, "A professional wrestler,"
And another said, "A veterinarian"
I was on the roll until another student stood up,
Looked me in the eyes and said,
"I want to be alive"

Now I can't let this slide
America a murdering place to live
Where by the age of five
Most children in my neighborhood are traumatized and desensitized
Walking over yellow tape on the first day of school
And we expect them to pay full attention,
Sit up straight and not act out like fools

They deserve a chance to live
But the root stems from controlling economic status
And their disgusting habits

Not to give a Damn about anyone or anything
That doesn't fall into their place
And this goes way beyond race

So after class the student and I advised a plan
To scholar this scholar with scholarships
To send him to college
Howard, Yale, Michigan State or a HBCU

This child will not be available
For the school to prison pipeline
No! This young king will utilize his mind
To get out the hood and off the block

No definite guarantees, but
He has a greater chance of not getting his wig pushed back
With his hands held high in the air by a badge
Or some dude posted up on the AVE
Who meant to hit but missed and clipped
The beautiful little girl dressed in pink
Walking home from Sunday school
Can you see her?
So please...in the name of her lifeless body
Think twice...before you load that next clip

America, a murderous place to live
That will gladly give you a uniform, some guns, food, shelter,
Heath insurance and prescriptions drugs
To help you represent where you live
Fighting for a cause that you don't quite comprehend
However the skilled media representatives
Will help us understand how day and night
Seeing the faces of dead men on the battlefield is a necessity
But not as important as the 823 murders that were committed
in NY and the D (Detroit) in 2016

It never ceases to amaze me
How we have a Chicago fire and PD
For the whole world to admire on HULU and regular TV
But they are never shown the real war zones
From every block where there's a HOT spot
That you cannot cross without witnessing a memorial
Or fearing for your life
Yet we fuel the fire when one of us are hit by uniform clip
But when we kill one another we sing a different song
A tune that's easily played out because that was my nigga
And in spite of it all I'mma go all out.

While another family mourns
A sister, brother, wife, husband, son, daughter,
Grandparents, cousins, mother and father torn,
Worn out can't sleep at night
She's trying to raise a family on her own
One child after the other, now she's alone
From birth a mother experiences the bond of attunement
With each and every child
To carry life in a womb is GOD's miracles and blessings
So please help me grasp the mind of a woman
Who was pushed so far beyond belief
To freeze her babies' bodies from head to feet?
Me, I was frightened to read or listen to the news
I mean, did she show any signs? Leave any clues?
Not our babies, they will not become a part
Of America's a murderous place to live

So, stop individualizing, start communicating face to face
Pay attention to those around you
You just might save a life
For we are all one Big Family
And it stills take a village to raise a child up right
Build their minds, bodies and spirits
To face this world properly to take over and fight
Each one teach one ladies and gentlemen…
Cause when it's all said and done America is still our home

COMMUNICATING COMMONALITY

Communicating commonality
Makes some people feel inadequately separate
From what they were taught by their loved ones
To what they really feel in their hearts
So I sit, watching, observing
How human beings have become so immune to death and violence

Yet everyone is silenced
By the reality of the tell a lie vision
That keeps our mind blurry
While we stay more interested in artist
Who could care less about the world we live in
And the stress we consume daily

But daily we just log on to social networks
Trying to find worth in other people's lives
Let me describe
How when I post a flick
I get about 200 more licks
I mean likes despite when I post about how
Israel Wants all Africans to take flight

Since 2010 Africans in Israel have been dehumanized
Despite that fact the controlled media continues
To sweep it under the rug
When will all of you around the world accept and understand
That every single living woman and man
Came from African descent
It was never meant for us to live as savages or slaves
With early arrivals to our graves

*** **Those We Honor** ***
Police Killings in 2015

Keith Childress (12-31-15)

Bettie Jones (12-25-15)

Kevin Matthews (12-23-15)

Leroy Browning (12-20-15)

Roy Nelson (12-19-15)

Miguel Espinal (12-8-15)

Nathaniel Pickett (11-19-15)

Tiara Thomas (11-18-15)

Cornelius Brown (11-18-15)

Chandra Weaver (11-17-15)

Jamar Clark (11-15-15)

Richard Perkins (11-15-15)

Stephen Tooson (11-12-15)

Michael L. Marshall (11-11-15)

Alonzo Smith (11-1-15)

Yvens Seide (10-31-15)

Anthony Ashford (10-27-15)

Lamontez Jones (10-20-15)

Rayshaun Cole (10-17-15)

Paterson Brown (10-17-15)

Christopher Kimble (10-3-15)

Junior Prosper (9-28-15)

Keith McLeod (9-23-15)

Wayne Wheeler (9-7-15)

India Kager (9-5-15)

Tyree Crawford (9-1-15)

James Carney, III (8-31-15)

Felix Kumi (8-28-15)

Wendell Hall (8-27-15)

Asshams Manley (8-14-15)

Christian Taylor (8-7-15)

Troy Robinson (8-6-15)

Brian Day (7-25-15)

Michael Sabbie (7-22-15)

Billy Ray Davis (7-20-15)

Samuel Dubose (7-19-15)

Darrius Stewart (7/17/15)

Albert Davis (7-17-15)

Sandra Bland (7-13-15)

Salvado Ellswood (7-12-15)

George Mann (7-11-15)

Jonathan Sanders (7-8-15)

Victo Larosa, III (7-2-15)

Kevin Judson (7-1-15)

Spencer McCain (6-25-15)

Kevin Bajoie (6-20-15)

Zamiel Crawford (6-20-15)

Jermaine Benjamin (6-16-15)

Kris Jackson (6-15-15)

Alan Craig Williams (6-13-15)

Ross Anthony (6-9-15)

Richard Gregor Davis (5-31-15)

Markus Clark (5-21-15)

Lorenzo Hayes (5-13-15)

De'Angelo Stallworth (5-12-15)

Dajuan Graham (5-12-15)

Brandon Glenn (5-6-15)

Reginald Moore (5-6-15)

Nuwnah Laroche (5-6-15)

Jason Champion (5-6-15)

Bryan Overstreet (4-28-15)

Terrance Kellom (4-27-15)

David Felix (4-25-15)

Lashonda Ruth Belk (4-24-15)

Gregory Daquan Harris (4-24-15)

Terry Lee Chatman (4-23-15)

William Chapman (4-22-15)

Samuel Harrell (4-21-15)

Freddie Gray (4-19-15)

Norman Cooper (4-19-15)

Brian Acton (4-18-15)
Darrell Brown (4-17-15)
Frank Shephard, III (4-15-15)
Walter Scott (4-4-15)
Donald "Dontay" Ivy (4-2-15)
Eric Harris (4-2-15)
Phillip White (3-31-15)
Dominick Wise (3-30-15)
Jason Moland (3-29-15)
Nicholas Thomas (3-24-15)
Denzel Brown (3-22-15)
Brandon Jones (3-19-15)
Askari Roberts (3-17-15)
Terrance Moxley (3-10-15)
Anthony Hill (3-9-15)
Bernard Moore (3-6-15)
Naeschylus Vinzant (3-6-15)
Tony Robinson (3-6-15)
Charly "Africa" Keunang, (3-1-15)
Darrell Gatewood (3-1-15)
Deontre Dorsey (3-1-15)
Thomas Allen, Jr. (2-28-15)

Terry Price, (2-20-15)
Calvon Reid (2-22-15)
Natasha McKenna (2-8-15)
Jeremy Lett (2-4-15)
Alvin Haynes (1-26-15)
Tiano Meton (1-22-15)
Andre Larone Murphy, Sr. (1-7-15)
Brian Pickett (1-6-15)
Leslie Sapp (1-6-15)
Matthew Ajibade (1-1-15)

Killed by Racist without a badge

Trayvon Martin (2-26-12)
Yusef Hawkins (8-23-89)
Willie Edwards (1-23-57)
James Chaney (6-21-64)
Michael Donald (3-20-81)
Michael Griffith (12-19-86)
James Byrd, Jr. (6-7-98)
Addie Mae Collins, Cynthia
Wesley, Carole Robertson,
Carol Denise McNair (9-15-63)
Emmitt Till (8-28-55)
(Witness Confessed to lying)

I will fight and write for you
I can't have it any other way
My ancestors' strength will never ever be taken away.

Every gunshot, plunger, every river,
Every Klansman that forced an African king and queen
To their early death
For every case the prosecutor refused to try
For every pickup truck that draaaaagggged an African's body

The savages from Howard Beach
Who are free to speak and live out their hate crimes
Nightsticks sexually assaulted, sodomized
And strip-searched to the core.
Enough is enough

Or shall I continue to speak
About your corrupt nation
That controls every media station and what they report

Oh! You thought it was all real
But they had this planned out way before they cut the deal
To make Donald Chump Cheetos or
Hilarious Connected Clinton
Our Next President

WHAT IF I TOLD YOU

What if I told you…
    I'm afraid to be happy because something hurtful and
    harmful comes attached to it?

What if I told you…
    Every time I loose someone I love I lose a piece of
    myself?

What if I told you…
    I love so strong with loyalty and need to see you on your
    successful life journey?

What if I told you…
    I have helped more people than I have hurt in this world?

What if I told you…
    I am connected to the universe and what I say think and
    feel comes to light?

What if I told you…
    I never knew who I was until I knew where my ancestors
    came from?

What if I told you…
   The word "mother fuc*er" came from slavery, at a time
   when devilish slave owners ripped Black sons from their
   mothers at birth; and when they were old enough were
   taken back to their mothers for entertainment—
   blindfolded and forced to have intercourse with the
   mothers—creating a MOTHER FUC**ING DAY!

What if I told you…
   Some of our youth could care less about life and
      more about fame, fortune, Netflix and chill?

What if I told you…
   I am disappointed in myself for not working the hardest
   and smartest every minute of my life?

What if I told you…
   The Black woman is God

What if I told you…
   I am beyond repulsed and disgusted but not surprised by
   what Blacks (aka African Americans) face as a nation?

What if I told you…
   Fake people, fake politicians and fake leaders equals
   Chaos in America?

What if I told you…
   This poem will never end because slavery should have
   never begun

What if I told you…
   Luke from *2 Live Crew* left a Trump Party, hosted by
   Trump because it was way outta control. Yes, that Luke.

What if I told you…
   Skinny jeans are not an attractive look for men at all, "ever!!"

What if I told you...
    Nate Parker and I lived in the same Los Angeles complex
    and his wife has been holding him down long before PRIDE,
    GREAT DEBATERS and BEYOND THE LIGHTS?

What if I told you...
    We are still enslaved in some way, shape, form or capacity

What if I told you...
    Religion has brainwashed us to worship white supremacy
    and that Nate Parker brought it to life in the cinema?

What if I told you...
    White supremacy is everywhere and in everything?

What if I told you...
    If you think they are going to let a Black president take
    charge for eight years and things wouldn't go insane
    afterwards, then you are lost?

What if I told you...
    There is only one type of disease (mucus) and all others
    are man-made, according to Dr. Sebi

What if I told you...
    Every positive Black organization and business
    has been infiltrated with a spy?

What if I told you...
    This election shows how desensitized we are to the worth
    and work of a woman?

What if I told you...
    Most people in NYC work to pay bills not live life?

What if I told you...
    Only eat fruits beginning with the #9 on the small sticker

What if I told you…
   Some countries of West Indies take a break during the
   day and everything shuts down to celebrate life?

What if I told you…
   All sports are fueled with some form of slavery, catering to
   men's egos and 90% of them involve running, chasing and
   or putting a ball into some type of hole? Think about it!

What if I told you…
   If a man does not honor his mother, then run away?

What if I told you…
   90% of the deodorant we use contains aluminum,
   which is directly connected to breast cancer?

What if I told you…
   Most people wear a daily mask and we have no idea
   who they really are?

What if I told you…
   I saw my first murder at the age of fourteen; and neither I
   nor the firefighters were trained in administering CPR, so
   we watched a man die?

What if I told you…
   More Caucasians (Whites) are on welfare than
   African Americans (Blacks); and that there are more Jews
   on welfare that receive more benefits than Blacks?

What if I told you…
   The school systems are failing our children?

What if I told you…
   The Lewinsky scandal existed to cover up the murder
   (alleged suicide) of Gary Web, the journalist who exposed
   government corruption and ties to drug cartels and more

HATE GROUPS

Hate groups you're a joke
Leaving smoking mirrors, we clearly see through you
You keep growing and growing
While we remain stronger, bolder, wiser, more responsible
And popular than your hate group will ever be

We don't wear sheets
Hide behind lawyers
Fake politicians, witnesses or police

And speaking of racists with guns
The life you live is a sad situation
There can't be any fun constantly tanning under the sun
While we are melanin rich

Don't forget in 1951
How doctors without consent
Stole the miraculous cells of Henrietta Lacks
A beautiful cancer patient
The doctors were impatient
Never got her permission to begin their mission
To open her up and become their study guide
Guiding us with dishonesty and constant lies

It doesn't get any better the more you read and learn
Watching TV; celebrities dancing with stars
Switching channels to every country
Having weapons of mass destruction
From the Tech Nine to that big booty that looks fine
We have completely lost our minds
And Henrietta Lacks cells are still alive to this day

STEPPING BACK

Stepping back looking at my reflection
I see dedication
Meditation, admiration and some trepidation
Traveling across many nations
NYC, LA, ATL, T&T, Turks & Caicaos
Dominican Republic, Michigan, Florida, Hawaii
Paris and Amsterdam

Now a closer step to the Motherland,
Meeting people in different places
Planes, trains, buses and stations
While trying to avoid encounters
With satanic type people across the nation

The Almighty has looked upon me in non-judgment
Brought me through this temple body that is sanctioned
To serve with an open heart with intellectual smarts

Like a child running track 5-10 miles back in the day
With a boyfriend trying to guide me
And losing himself along the way
No father presence to present presents
or words of wisdom and knowledge

Learning at an early age
The meaning of the word homage
My mother, a queen working to feed and clothe me solo
Raising me up right while baby sitters became family
Still on speed dial to this current day
And will quickly take a flight to assist in any possible way

Raised in Grace Baptist Church, taught and learned the gospel
Went to the streets for some guidance and understanding
Was introduced to positive big sisters along the way

Became street smart with a few tussles
"A" slammed a girl back in the day

Still running track, traveling to Queens with Aunt Mary
Weekend stays turned into weekly overlays
Eric, Sabrina, Uncle Jean
Eric feeding me his fav
Franks and beans every day
Family love took over in a special way

Mom still working BFF back in Brooklyn
But we still kept things tight during those days and nights
No cells, Facebook, or Instagram
Thrilled about it, which you probably don't understand

Working, in school and always staying busy
I realize now, New York City
Is just that type of place
You spend soon as you leave your home
Transportation, food, all due
Two or three jobs to make it through

High, low and middle class citizens
Some turn a blind ear and eye
Pretending not to see, hear or understand
The gentrification of the economical plan
That has taken hold on the demands
To keep the rich richer and poor poorer
While we argue over Oscars and Chumps
An ignorant distraction that cannot endure
Or help lift us up and out of these dangerous situations
It will take the Nation to pause for a real cause
Of self-evaluation

Got to be willing to face the truth
With the lies Melon consumption,
These thieves use contamination

Stealing minds and body parts
The need to conspire and permanently retire
People that look like us—damn it, it's so hard to trust

FEAR: "**False Education Appearing Real**"
Stay with me
When a child's not giving opportunities to explore
Traveling higher places not being ignored
Not telling what will be accomplished or obtained
You imagine not being able to fly or soar

Working many jobs for brands I didn't own Nike,
Victoria's Secret, Elite Model Management

Flipped it to Angelic Kreations, Inc.
Been in existence for over ten years
2004 and 2006 calendars displaying sexy and
classy Don't have to be naked
Just dedicated, loving and passionate

Bachelor's and Master's from Michigan
Public speaking aka Forensics fit the bill assisting me through
Persuasion, Dramatic Interpretation, POI's, Duo's
Communication Analyst and Poetry to

Drawing them in with my words
A powerful gifted tool
One of the many blessings God's guided me through

The more positive I am the more I understand
Giving my life to GOD who's already ordained the
plan For this moment right here right now
For us together no mistakes made
Only uncertainty can complicate and cause doubts
About what the future holds
The flesh is weak looking to be feed

When I felt like slipping while grieving
I decided to take hold of myself
Allowing spirits to lead me
Through the heartache and pain
Revealing my true family, friends and support team

Learning that one's presence is their present
With heartfelt opened arms
Grateful, encouraged and blessed to see another healthy day
Accepting how this is just another chapter
Next up the Motherland "AFRICA"

ᘒᘖ

____

Dedicated To Those Called Home To Glory Too Soon

____

ᘒᘖ

THE ONE THAT WENT AWAY TOO SOON

The one that went away too soon
The skies opened up for her to bloom
With the stars that shine to brighten up the night
She was called home this Holiday season
Leaving us empty trying to explain and reason

With the spirit of God who's looking upon us
Morning, afternoon, dawn till dusk

Forgive us Father for we have all done wrong
In the midst of it all trying to be; I mean stay strong
As she diligently organized, prioritized, authorized, daily,
weekly, monthly, yearly successful tasks
For students, faculty and staff

Ensuring positive outcomes and lessons
Learned that will last a lifetime
It's kindergarten and middle school
That shape our children's minds
Thanks Mrs. Fung job well done

Your spirit
Your memory lives on as we pray
For your family and love ones to stay strong
Holding on to your memories
Your legacy at P.S. 306
Your presence is already missed
You held the keys to many doors
That open the hearts of children
Even on their rough days
They couldn't stay away and loved calling your name

The one who went away too soon
When the sky meets the moon
And just when you think you have it all figured out

Screaming, shouting
It's time to take a moment sort things out
To bring forth kindness, love, caring, understanding
Making it a daily routine as we strive to improve
The conditions that have us conditioned to be nasty, mean and rude

Unable to love and respect themselves or one another
A woman's work is never done,
She's watching over the sons and daughters
All the children in a heavenly place
Where she's probably already in a position to lead
When you spend time on earth changing lives
Your family can rest assure knowing
That her heart and soul rests at peace

Peacefully accepting the greatness
That's attached to all her good deeds
On planet earth
Adia, Zion and Solama
She lives on in you, believes and is counting on you
To carry on her legacy making it through
Fulfilling your dreams and goals
You are all beautiful, talented, educated,
Spitting image of your mother it's true
None of us know exactly what you're going through
But if allowed we would like to wrap our arms around, you
Tell you we love you
Care and will be here for you
Plus, you have an entire community to support and pray with you
Because we feel the pain

It's a heavy hurtful load that's sometimes ready to explode
The Almighty has a plan in place
Have faith in His grace
For blessings and merciful times lie ahead
For it has been written quoted and said

God only gives us what we can handle not dismantle
So when the beautiful sun sets at night
We are reminded of its Bold, Bright and Beautiful Women
Who get things done right
The ones who went away too soon
Mrs. Fung we love and miss you

MARY COLEMANN
Died of Breast Cancer

Born Leader, Loyal and Lovable
Thanks for all your blessings and hard word especially your daughters.
You set an exemplary example for women to follow
Carrying yourself with dignity and class
A LEO Queen of course you never asked
For a handout or free ride
Empowering, helping, encouraging others you never let that slide
Working with others to help spread kindness
My dear LEO Queen born on the 18th of August you were the finest
At opening your home, heart and ears to family and strangers
Listening, educating and nurturing at its best
The Family has been strong since your departure
Holding on, growing, showing, not knowing what the future holds
But "One Thing For Sure And Two Things For Certain"
And definitely true
God is as good as gold and so are you
Continue watching over us always Mama Colemann, we need you!!

AUNT BANI

Famous 60's-70's Model Killed By Knife

Aunt Bani where are you now?
Is your soul not at rest
Because your murderer has not been found
1974 was the year while your sister was giving birth to me
Someone slit your throat from ear to ear

Never gave a thought to what it might do
To those who loved you or would never get to know you
That "mf" must have really been obsessed with you Your
sexy curves and brown caramel skin
High cheeks bones and slender long legs
You were rocking the Halle
Before she even knew she was a Berry
You were the first African American woman
Painted on the walls of New York City mean streets

Robbed of the chance to give birth
My mom couldn't handle the hurt
Pushed it so far back in her mind that I became blind
Scared to open my eyes and see the beauty of you

Heard you used to sell jewelry
At a store in the village to be exact
Bet you was slaying flawless queens on the scene
Was breaking modeling barriers
Not realizing I would follow in your footsteps
Dreaming to be just like you

Wanting to be loved and appreciated just like you
Independent and strong just like you
But I'm scared to love
'Cause I don't want to be murdered just like you

Aunt Bani, I'm carrying you with me daily
Waiting for a sign
Trying to fight the fear
Of love that lives inside of me

YOU

There is no one like you
No one could ever replace you
You never lost touch with any of us
From Brooklyn, Queens, Atlanta and LA
You were the true definition of a brother whom I could Trust

You drove the fastest cars
Traveled and dined at the fanciest bars
Having meetings with stars
That later gave you their full attention
As they waited for you to mention
Where you would be hanging out next

Your heart was huge you gave, shared, never pretended
Not to care about how your loved ones were really feeling
Our bonding time was my healing
Your jokes, your style, you plucking my nerves
From High School
When no one else could understand you or I
But we already knew we would take this world on
And truly live doing things the right way—our way
I often reminisce on those days
Even when I would be pissed at you
You still didn't stay away
'Cause you knew I was cooking for the holidays

Since your departure I try harder to make sure
The ones I cherish on earth don't give up or settle
Brandi and I have built a lifelong Bond
While Chase the King is growing intelligent
Intellectual and strong
Still hurts that you're gone
But I made a promise to hold on
Holding back tears as I write this poem
While I build this Empire to inspire
The future generations of youth you were always true

Life is a part of death
Death is a part of life
What we do in between
Do it like my brother Mike
Live it Right on your own terms
With no limitations, few rules, no regrets
While reaching out to strangers, family, friends
And love ones being there to heal and hold them down
When it hurts

PAT! PUT! PUP!

Killed By Police Gunshots

Pat! Put! Pup! What's Dat Sound, Son? In the Hot Sun?
Sounds Like a Gun Son
There Falls another Mother's Son
This Son was Young and Strong
Big, Black and Brown—Michael Brown

A Mother's Son Laid on the Hot Pitch
Like a Fish Out of Water
Dead from the Lead of a Cop trained to Slaughter

Young Black Men?
How many gone? 10,000 and ten?

Sorry Mommy Says the Tainted Grand Jury
Your Darling was a Demon
Head Bent Down
Ready to Charge the Badge of our own Dear Son
Darren Wilson

We trained our Darren to make your Hood Barren
Shoot Your Sons even if there is no Threat.
Wilson's Ounce of Fear is worth Your Son's Death?
Wait! "Michelle Alexander" You Did Say
So Black Blood that Flow is the New Jim Crow

Yes, we now drive the Bus. We sit in the Front
But still treat us like the Animals they Love to Hunt

Dehumanized by Blue Eyes with a Gun
Hands Up Means Nothing
They are just having Fun....with that Mother's Son

This is not THRILLING
A Billion Chinese
Only 12 Killings
By Cops per year

But Dear or Dear Don't they hear that The Sound
In America the Beautiful we filling that quota
With Black Mothers, Black Sons and Daughters

DEMARIUS REED

Killed By Gunshot

Can you hear me? Can you see us now?
Demarius Reed
Another King taken from us too soon

Everyone here knows your name
Demarius, I will never equate death with fame
We here at Eastern Michigan University are mourning for you
We cannot just say rest in peace
'Cause you were supposed to be safe in these Ypsilanti streets

Violence and murder been spreading amongst us far too long
Taken from us last year, they told us not to worry
Not to be scared
Keep telling us to be strong
And that there's a point to it all
We must come together to weather this storm
Watch over us carefully cause it's hard staying strong

The Football team at EMU will cherish your memory for life
A student on the rise
Who knew death at EMU would be your demise
May your family, friends and girlfriend mourn peacefully
And keep you close to their hearts
I can only image the challenges they're dealing with
Trying to keep from falling apart

They finally caught the cowards with no heart
Prayerfully, this poem will resonate in someone's brain
Enough to drive us all revolutionarily insane
Proclaiming to do better and be better as a people
In making a change from violence to love
Where our African brothers and sisters reign

DR. KING

Killed by gunshot on April 4, 1968

HEY, DR. KING
Are you resting better now that you have your queen?
Things are still mean out here on these streets
We are still at a place of defeat
Have you seen all the streets named after you?
Dr. King, after this poem I hope you're not feeling blue

Chicago and Africa have the highest murder rate
I know your wish, your dream and goal
Was for things to get better
Look at us now, a few generations later

Your born day is a known National Holiday
Dr. King, it seems like the jails have replaced the slave trade
We keep murdering each other, one by one, two by two
Praying over our loved ones and relatives
As we put them in the grave

Dr. King, did you see what happen the other day?
Another EMU student's life been taken away
Demarius is your soul resting next to Dr. King?
Can we take a moment of silence for you
And every university student
Who have lost their lives while enrolled in a school

Let us close our eyes…ok, cool
Dr. King, I'm confused
But more so concerned
My mind and body yearns
For a word to say and my smile to give way
Can I help someone have a better day?
Or are they feeling what I feel, in the same way

Dr. King, did you always see the good in men and women
Always willing to lend a hand for the struggle
You know, haters are still trying to find your flaws
Even surveillance recording of you dropping draws
They still giving your boy Jesse a hard time
With his mistress flaws

Dr. King, I wonder if I could get those same people
To count how many doors were opened
With your mind, body and strength
Your persuasion was amazing
Your delivery, impeccable
Your tone, alluring
Your swag, adoring

Dr. King, were you with us
The night the Trayvon Martin verdict came down
Did you know the outcome anyway?
Knowing ignorance will say, "This is payback for O.J."
Why do they use the courts in this way?
Goated by the spirit of hierarchy

Learning to understand its richer complications
Humans idealize perfection that doesn't exist
In order to retain this structure
Dominant power in a society seeks to sustain the struggle
Amongst marginalized groups
Pitting one oppressed group against one another
Allowing those in power to retain power
Unchallenged because the oppressed groups are preoccupied
Fighting amongst each other

Dr. King, look what they did to you—you, the KING
Dr. Martin Luther King, Jr., after sharing your dream
Wonder what they would do to a Queen who dared to dream?
So, I keep to myself, holding things in and bottled up

Writing has become my weapon of mass destruction
A prescription for my health
A passionate addiction for uplifting people and changing lives

Thanks, Dr. King for caring
Thanks for sharing
How to love
I know you are probably saying, "Hey ya'll still marching!"
"Better stop playing and get into formation"
"Cause we are the creators of this nation!"

ZENO

Words cannot express the pain
What can your *Man Up* sisters say
Your mother has received her wings
And gone home to glory, resting peacefully as she lay

We get far in life on our mother's love
Even further in embracing and reminiscing
Of her motherly touch

Beautiful, kind, sweet, queen
Remember she raised you, so she had to be strong
Now it's your turn, the baton is in your hand
Keep your head held high, for the Most High has a plan

Our mothers are with us always
First, in her lifetime and then forever in our memory
So, when the wind blows and shakes the trees
From this day forward
Breathe in, close your eyes and say,
"My angel of a mother is walking with me forever"

REST IN PEACE AUNT SALLIE

Rest in Peace, Aunt Sallie
As the trees blow and the winds sing
Aunt Sallie has closed her eyes to dream.

Filling the sky with another special star at night
On Sunday she rose with the morning sun
She raised so many of us on Scheneck Avenue
I'm just a testimony of one
Apt 3-D will never be the same

But allow me to summarize a few of the good memories
that go with this pain:
Atari, Monopoly, Mary Jane Girls, M.J. and Cabbage Patch Kids
She introduced us to many things
Teaching us how to shape our womanhood and live

Venus and Chan, thanks for sharing your mom
Her loving bond was so strong that she touched many lives
There are a few others I must mention in this poem
Carmen, Ebony, Keisha, Velma, Karisha,
Nicole and Meka Luv
"I didn't know you moved," a little inside joke
From Aunt Sally to her girls—our crew
Let's not forget how she held down housing patrol
And her cooking was always, I mean always, good for the soul

Speak your mind
Stand strong for what you believe
Love your family and yourself through each and every season
Always reach out in love, compassion and understanding
A proud sister, aunty, mother, godmother, life coach,
Grandmother, great grandmother and friend…
In our the hearts you live on with loved ones

And other 857 family members and friends
The perfect star shining
Watching over us in Heaven

EMMANUEL SUPREME

Keep your head held high with a smile on your face
Your father has reached his resting place
I'm not going to say some days or nights won't be rough
But just remember his spirit is watching over you, along with
God's touch

Brooklyn needs a positive change not more violence
This sh*t is a crying shame
For all the days you feel like things are coming apart
Keep your dad's memory close to your heart
Stay strong, demand respect and be smart

You're a queen of African descent
And it was meant for you to rise above it all
Don't allow anything or anyone to be your downfall
Surround yourself with good people
You can trust, learn from and have fun with

Your father is watching and waiting
Guiding you with his love under the sun
Keep your head held high with a smile on your face

Emmanuel Supreme, your dad was a real good man
He's been called home to rest in a much better place
And he would want nothing better than the best for you
His Princess

MY SISTER, I MISS YA

A Dear True Friend Who Died Of Breast Cancer

My sister I miss ya, you're now with the Lord
So, chatting with you now is truly to hard
So, with these words I write to you up above
To celebrate your life, my dearest friend, Meka Luv

Thanks for being the angel who lived with us here on earth
Your smile, your laughter, your mischievous little mirth
All the fun that we cherished, for all that its worth
You brought joy to our childhood with that little smirk

Fleeting memories of hot summers
Learning new dances from street drummers
Going to summer camp with your cousin Tyra
We shared lunches and munches, and all things we admire

Meka Luv, my dear, one thing is sure
One day we'll all be knock, knock, knocking
On Heaven's door
But why do I feel this vast empty space
I closed my eyes and keep seeing your face
That smirk, that joke, that sisterly grace

My tears are restrained trying my best to maintain
I call Ricky, Tanya, Nya and Dawn's name
Think hip hop, funk, gospel and soul like the song
"Celebrate good times, come on!"

My mama used to say,
Girl you'd be lucky to find five real friends in a lifetime
Some will come, some will go, some will stay like fine wine
Meka Luv, I was the best of yours
And you were the best of mine

From Brooklyn to Queens to the Bronx
We used to dine in restaurants
Cafés and street fairs in the hood
Two skinny fat ladies in the mood for good food

You touched everyone in a positive way
At home, at work and on the streets, everyday
Kids at Kwanzaa, at school or at play
Touched papa's and mama's on their special day
Friends, fans, family and great birthdays

Sorry I missed you before your last flight
But God in His wisdom, His timing and might
Lays down His red carpet to Heaven's great door
Angels like you, who are so kind and pure
Are called home to glory with no more pain to endure
So please say "Hi" to your mama, papa, Aunt Sallie,
The Browns, Niesha and others who left us so soon
You now join the great ones that God called home before forty

Like Martin, Malcolm, Aaliyah and Bob Marley
Gone too soon but an early heavenly arrival
One dream, one love and one in a million
You loved all of us by any means necessary

Your faith never wavered
You fought a great fight
You were blessed and highly favored
So God made it just right
For you to make Heaven, your posh new home
My gosh, how I'll miss you my dearest Meka Luv

You lived your life like a champion
Caring for everyone with all your heart
Now that you are gone, we will miss you
As your soul from this world departs

SAY HER NAME: "KORRYN GAINES"

Sister Killed By Police On 8/1/2016

Say her name
KORRYN GAINES

Say her name again
KORRYN GAINES

Gaines was gaining our attention
Without failure to mention
Why she was so furious
Some still curious about her actions alone or with her child

Said she was dangerous, running wild
With a death wish she put on herself
While cowards always calling for help
When "white supremacy" radicalizes us into this state of mind
Are you "mo-fo's" deaf, dumb or just blind?

Centuries and decades of slavery war crimes
Against us has made me question my trust
As I lust for the day to be free
Free of mind, body, and spirit ya see
Back in the days when we were only physically enslaved
And some great Queens, Kings, and Goddesses fought back

There were many folk that said, "Man, that sh*t is wack."
"We can't do that, we must obey the law."
"Otherwise, they will expose and kill us all."

HARRIET TUBMAN said it best: "I had reasoned this out in
my mind; there was one of two things I had a right to, liberty
or death; if I could not have one, I would have the other for no
man should take me alive." (Larson, n.d.)

"I had crossed the line. I was free; but there was no one to
welcome me to the land of freedom. I was a stranger in a
strange land…" (Harriet Tubman Historical Society, 2016).

Harriet Tubman and Korryn Gaines took a stand and
demanded there freedom by any means

So these naysayers are the same slaves
Harriett Tubman spoke about ya see
The cowards of this day amaze me
Still can't see through the "bullsh*t fu*kery"
Displayed on the internet, social media or tell-a-lie TV

Man, listen to me, our minds are almost gone
We been singing, saying and marching to
The same old tired ass songs "Drawn"

We are the only race and culture
That will publicly stand up against one another
Folks keep asking me
"How long you going to wait to become a mother?"
As if, I am not Mother Earth since birth

My interest and purpose might not be in line with yours
But I was sent by the spirits and God to do more
Hours of writing, teaching, listening, speaking and uplifting
Spending less time babysitting a man—no disrespect intended
But when it's time to go to war
While others have children and loved ones to care for
I am my own boss
The person with the least to lose is the most dangerous
And I'm not trying to be famous from a hash tag or body bag

I'm sick to my soul down to my core
Yes, I want more positivity for our people
And we already proved you wrong
You know we can fly, stay fly, got swag and all

Saw a video of my African brothers and sisters
Who built a music studio from trees, water bottles,
boxes, wood that's all
We are the greatest to have ever done it all.
Even when our backs are pinned against the wall

So on that day, sis had enough
Was she rough, tough, ride or die
Naw, Korryn Gaines was a modern day Harriett Tubman
Who stood up to right the wrong of our people
And on that day, Korryn Gaines was given her wings to fly
And for that reason alone
You need to say her name
KORRYN GAINES
Say her name
KORRYN GAINES

UNCLE AARON "THE CHAMP" YELVERTON

Died of Throat Cancer on Oct 29, 2015

Born the Best Champ in so many ways
Your name rings a bell since the great bible days
Aaron, the high priest
Moses, the big brother, fighting pharaohs and fears
It didn't really matter
From boxer to ball player
Born August 27
Seems you dribbled your way back to heaven
I know angels are waiting for heroes like you
But let me celebrate because the best champs are few

Remember at age 3 how you fell out of the bed?
The nurses and doctors thought you were dead
But God added 77 more years to build the right champ
A life that beamed like light from a bright lamp
Even brighter when you laughed or grinned

We made a great team 'cause you taught me to win
You ran the best race with wisdom and wit
Stood in God's grace until it was time to quit

Only one brother out of three bold fine sisters
With enough love to beat all the gold that glitters
For Aunt Odessa, Aunt Bani, and my Mom

For family and friends, wherever they come from
We celebrate your life because you made us all proud
Through stress and strife, you still laughed out loud
With jokes over dinner, you taught me life's game
You even played ball with legends like Wilt Chamberlain

So from me, your niece, Karen, on your home going day
Thanks for sharing a peace and love that will never fade away
Thanks, Uncle Aaron
My friend and the best champ in the game
Rest in perfect peace in God's great hall of fame

ART by SERENITY GONZALEZ

The following student artwork was submitted by Serenity Gonzalez of P.S. 306

REFERENCES

Larson, Kate Clifford. (n.d.). *Harriet Tubman Biography*. Retrieved from http://www.harriettubmanbiography.com /harriet-tubman-myths-and-facts.

Harriet Tubman Historical Society. (2016). *Harriet Tubman Quotes*. Retrieved from http://www.harriet-tubman.org /quotes.

Economy, Peter. (2015, Mar. 20). Inc.com. *19 Empowering Quotes from Oprah Winfrey*. Retrieved from http://www.inc.com/peter-economy/oprah-winfrey-19-inspiring-power-quotes-for-success.

https://www.washingtonpost.com/graphics/national/police-shootings/

ANGELIC KREATIONS
Poetry Between Sisters

www.ingramcontent.com/pod-product-compliance
Lightning Source LLC
Chambersburg PA
CBHW071023180726
48291CB00004B/1590